Clodagh Corcoran was
She worked for a time
children's bookshop in
Secretary of the Feder
Groups, a Director of Books for Your
member of the Yorkshire Arts Association literature panel. In 1977 she founded the Mother Goose Award for children's book illustration.

After her divorce she returned to Dublin in 1981. As a member of the Executive of the Irish Council for Civil Liberties, she established a Working Party in 1984, funded by the Department of Health, to look at the problem of child sexual abuse in Ireland. In 1985 she edited and produced an Information Pack on child sexual abuse, in association with the Health Education Bureau. In 1986 she established the Sanctuary Trust, to give help and support to the victims of child sexual abuse and their families.

She is currently working on a further book.

TAKE CARE!

PREVENTING CHILD SEXUAL ABUSE

CLODAGH CORCORAN

POOLBEG

A Paperback Original
First published 1987 by
Poolbeg Press Ltd.,
Knocksedan House,
Swords, Co. Dublin, Ireland

Cover design by Steven Hope
Typeset by Busby Typesetting & Design,
Exeter, England.
Printed by The Guernsey Press Ltd.,
Vale, Guernsey, Channel Islands.

Contents

Acknowledgements

I want to pay tribute to all those who have shared their experience of sexual abuse with me. To those who survived the experience, and those who are still struggling to come to terms with it. To the mothers who were bretrayed, and the fathers who had to cope with the knowledge that a brother, son or friend had chosen to sexually abuse his children.

I want also to specifically acknowledge the help and support of the following:

Cathy Alborough, Breda Allen, Ruth Corcoran, Brendan Dowling, the Doyle Family, Emily Driver, Audrey Droisen, Michelle Elliott, Olwen Ellis, the Fitzpatrick Family, Paul Griffiths, Val Jackson, Paula Lambert, Jim Lynch, Michael Monaghan, Sarah Nelson, Pauline O'Byrne, Fiona Purdy, Corinna Reynolds, Jean Rowe, Valerie Smith, Rosemary Stones, Michael Teff, Chris Whelan.

For Pauline Beegan, Yvonne Whelan and Amy Garvey for practical help, advice, support and love.

I remember my silent bedroom,
in smiling infancy, enchanted
by my wandering mind. How I
triumphed in victorious battles.
I my army, against two thousand.
Fought me, the strongest fiercest soldier,
So with glorious power, unwitnessed,
I struck the man ten
thousand times . . .
''A battle in clouds . . .''
My mother would say.

Yet fully revenged I was.
Imbattled in my mind.

Finbar Murray Cristobal

Preface

Why do some children become victims, and some become victimisers? This question has exercised me for a number of years now. I came to the reluctant conclusion that, if there is an adult who wishes to gratify his desires by sexually abusing a child, he will do so and no power on earth will stop him. The answer appears to be in limiting the damage such abuse can cause by giving our children permission to protect themselves. Providing our children with information about their rights, their bodies and personal safety is, for many of us, entering unfamiliar territory. We are empowering them and at the same time identifying ourselves as their allies.

As adults, we control and define our children's reality. Not only are they in the position of being physically smaller than most of the people around them, but they are emotionally, financially, psychologically and physically dependent on us as well. If we tell them they cannot paint or dance or sing, they will grow up firmly believing these things. If we tell them that what they feel or think is not important to us, they will grow up denying their right to trust their feelings and instincts.

All adults share a common experience. We were all of us once children. For some, childhood was much shorter than for others. For many of us, it is too painful to recall how vulnerable and helpless we were in childhood.

Teaching our children prevention strategies will not be enough to make the world a safer place to grow up in, but it will be a start. Despite our teaching, some children will still be abused. It will not be their fault. It is never their fault. They are without power in an adult world.

The children are,
everyone's heirs,
everyone's business,
everyone's future.

Marge Piercy, *Woman on the Edge of Time*

Introduction

The legend of Saint Dymphna

Once upon a time a beautiful princess lived on an island where her mother and father were Queen and King. The name of this princess was Dymphna, and from her birth she had been an amazing child, in beauty, sweetness, and cleverness.

Dymphna's father, King Coninck, was a cruel man and a pagan. As Dymphna grew older, she understood that the Queen disagreed with the king about many things. For one thing, the Queen was a Christian, and Dymphna too began to learn Christianity from the hermit Gerebernus who lived in a hut in the forest.

One day the Queen became ill. On Christmas Eve, just before she died, she called Dymphna and Gerebernus to her and said, ''My daughter, I am no longer able to keep you under my protection. You must make your own decisions now. Gerebernus, try to guide her, with God's help.'' After that, the Queen died.

On losing his Queen, King Coninck sank into a black chagrin, becoming more and more cruel and stranger than ever. His counsellors, trying to cheer him, suggested that he seek a new Queen. And so he sent his soldiers throughout the land searching for someone worthy to be his Queen, someone as beautiful, as sweet, and as clever as was his dead wife. Alas, no such person could be found. When his messengers returned, the pagan King's mood became even blacker. Then a demon spoke to him. ''What you seek is near you,'' said the demon. King Coninck, glancing up, saw his daughter, Dymphna. "There is the living image of your dead wife," the demon said. "She alone is worthy to be the Queen of Ireland."

The next day he asked Dymphna to be his wife. When she refused he thought, "She says this because she is shy, still a young maiden. She will come around to my view soon enough. It is the only reasonable thing we can do, now that the Queen is dead."

Each day Coninck made his proposal anew, at times stroking her body and using sweet flattery, at other times explaining why his way was right, and at other times shouting, threatening, and waving his sword in a rage.

At last Dymphna could bear it no longer and went to the hermit Gerebernus for advice. "I wish my mother were here," she said. Gerebernus thought for a long time and, at last, he said, "There is no way out except to run. All I can offer to do is run with you." The hermit told Dymphna that to gain time she should ask the King to give her forty days in which to make up her mind about the marriage.

When Coninck heard this, he was overjoyed. He showered Dymphna with presents, and gave her dozens of fine silk dresses. "I will often be away from the castle," she told him. The King imagined that she was preparing for the wedding feast. In reality she was preparing to fly.

One day she went out on her white horse and did not return. She met Gerebernus and an old couple who had been friends of her mother. They ran their horses as far as the sea where Gerebernus had a boat ready. "My Princess," he said, "I do not know how to navigate, so I cannot tell you where this boat will take us. Do you still want to go?" Dymphna nodded and got into the boat. It was very cold and the sea was full of storms.

It was not until several days had passed that the servants in the castle dared to tell Coninck that his daughter had disappeared. First, he had his soldiers search for Dymphna throughout his own kingdom. When he found that Gerebernus too was missing, Coninck decided that it was

Gerebernus who had caused all of his troubles. "This hermit turned my wife against me, and probably poisoned her into the bargain. Now he has turned my dear Dymphna against me, and has taken her away." Coninck gathered a large army and began to search for Dymphna through all Ireland and then across the seas.

Miraculously, Dymphna's boat reached shore at the busy port of Antwerp, in Belgium. People came to stare at the old hermit and at the beautiful princess who wore torn, sodden, silken rags. She bought food for her friends with the Irish coins she had with her. Because she was beautiful, merchants "sold" her the food, even though her Irish coins had no value in Antwerp. "Let us keep going," said Gerebernus. "There are too many people here."

They walked for many days into the forest. After a long while, they came to a shrine dedicated to Saint Martin in a lonely place with only fifteen houses nearby. The village was called Gheel (or Geel, pronounced like a *gale* of wind). Gerebernus liked Saint Martin, so they stopped and built a hut near the shrine. They lived there in peace for about three months.

Meanwhile Coninck and his soldiers searched for Dymphna, moving out in ever-widening circles from Ireland. In Antwerp, the King heard of the beautiful girl and the hermit who had arrived in a boat. Coninck sent his men to comb the countryside for more news.

It was Coninck himself who sat down to dinner one night at the inn at Gheel. "Oh, I cannot take this kind of money from you," said the woman who had served him. "I take these from the girl who lives with the hermit in the forest, but only because she is mad. I do it out of charity. Mad as a hatter she is, but lovely. Why, she says her father wants her to be his wife. She imagines it all, of course. She tells me that we must keep all this a secret. Poor girl. She believes, in her madness, that her father is still searching for her."

Coninck drew his sword and ran toward the hut in the forest. His soldiers followed. The woman at the inn was left holding another one of those strange unlucky coins.

It was the end of May now, and warm and light in the evenings. Gerebernus saw the soldiers coming and went to the door, hoping to shield Dymphna from them. ''You are the enemy,'' said Coninck, seeing Gerebernus. ''I will kill you and be free.''

Dymphna came to stand at the side of her confessor. ''Please, for the love you have for me, do not kill him.''

''And what will you do for me if I spare your friend?'' said the King, reaching out to fondle her breasts. ''What little favour will you do for your father then?'' Gerebernus pushed the King away. ''The time has come to speak plainly, my King. No pacts with the devil are allowed. What you have proposed violates all rules of men and God.''

The King spoke again. ''Will you have me, Dymphna? In exchange for his life?''

''Never,'' said Dymphna.

As always, the passionate lust of the King was very near to becoming a passionate rage. ''You will be Queen of Ireland, or you will die,'' he said.

''My father,'' she answered, ''I simply cannot.''

He nodded as before, but this time no soldier moved. He lifted his chin, his eyes blazing. Still nothing happened. At last, one soldier walked over to Dymphna. He raised his sword. Then let it fall again. He could not kill her.

Coninck strode over to where she stood. With his own sword, he cut off the head of his daughter.

Dymphna was surprised to find that after all that she was still thinking. Coninck had done all he could to stop her thinking, but even this last had not succeeded. She was going upward, very fast, and Gerebernus was with her. She stretched out her arm to hug her mother. ''Dear Mother,'' said Dymphna, ''soon we will be together, but now I must find a way to bring Father with us.''

Dymphna pointed down to where her father, the King, was trampling and hacking at what he could see of Dymphna and of Gerebernus. His demon had now gained possession over his self. Coninck slavered and howled, trotted in circles, and kept spinning his sword above his head. His soldiers backed away from him in horror.

Dymphna, who was learning to fly with more control now, glided down to hover behind the woman at the inn. ''What have I done?'' the woman began to think. ''I thought she was just a mad, silly girl, but she was fighting for her life. How can I make up for what I have done?'' Just then King Coninck came wandering in. Coninck howled at the door, then fell to the floor and settled down to writhing like a snake, and hissing. The woman at the inn went to him. ''Perhaps I can care for this poor creature. He is guilty of much but so am I. I will try to give him the care that I did not give to his child. This one I will treat as one of my own family, not as someone to ridicule or to point the finger at, but as someone who truly belongs with us.''

Dymphna saw clearly now the demon riding upon her father's back. It looked like a small dragon with horns. She was amazed that she had never seen it before. She took the sword from her father's hand. The demon knew that she had recognised him and ran to hide under the bed. Coninck collapsed into the arms of the innkeeper. Dymphna kept stalking the demon. She hunted him for nine days before she caught him and stabbed him to death with her father's sword.

All this happened almost thirteen hundred years ago. Still today, if you see a picture of Saint Dymphna, she will be holding her father's sword and standing on the head of a vicious-looking demon. Gerebernus became a saint too, and now he has long conversations with his friend, Saint Martin, every day. In memory of Saint Dymphna, today the families of Gheel still take in those who are possessed or deranged and help them to get well. Dymphna still helps to heal such people, as she helped her father. It is said that madness can be cured if one stays for nine days in Dymphna's church. Today, fathers still make passionate, demonic proposals to their daughters, and the daughters must try and find a way to say no. This is about as easy as sprouting wings. Dymphna and Gerebernus still wonder if they could have found a simpler way to do it.

Reprinted with permission from *Sexual Abuse: Incest Victims and their Families* by Jean M. Goodwin et al (PSG Publishing Company Inc., Mass, 1982).

1 What is child sexual abuse?

''We are seldom prepared for the reactions of others to the news that our child has been sexually assaulted. Seeing their shock and denial gives us a visual image of our own initial feelings. However, we can't tolerate their asking; ''Are you sure it happened?''; ''Couldn't she be exaggerating?'' ''He's always had a great imagination, are you sure he didn't make it up?''; ''She seems fine, how could that have happened?'' When others accept the reality, we are then confronted with *their* fears. We are looking to them for support, and they are telling us how frightened they are for themselves and their children. If we respond with anger and annoyance, they in turn respond by apologising and feeling guilty. They then ask us what they can do, and we don't know what to tell them.''

Flora Colao and Tamar Hosansky,
Your Children Should Know

Traditionally, child sexual abuse has been defined as a "problem" within certain types of family: families living in rural areas, families where the mother is not a "good" mother, Catholic families, families living in areas where there is a high density population and poor housing, families where the father had poor schooling, is unemployed, and has a drink problem. Few researchers have found cases of incest among respectable, affluent middle-class populations, mainly because these groups are better able to cover up the problem and more significantly, because research has been generally carried out in working-class areas amongst the working-class population.

There are no boundaries

Unfortunately, it has recently been shown that the sexual abuse of children knows no class, racial or cultural boundaries. Young girls and boys are victimised in all societies. Their family circumstances for the most part are irrelevant, because abuse may happen outside the home as well as inside it. To condone it on the grounds that it is happening inside the home and is therefore no one else's business is to admit to a tolerance of criminal acts against children for no better reason than that those committing the crimes are parents.

Having treated well over 300 cases of sexual abuse within the family, social worker Susan Forward concluded that her cases represented every economic, cultural, racial, educational, religious and geographical background. The abusers were doctors, policemen, prostitutes, secretaries, artists and merchants. They were heterosexual, bisexual and homosexual. They were happily married, and four-times divorced, they were emotionally stable and they had multiple personalities. *(Betrayal of Innocence)*.

A true definition

A true definition of sexual abuse would focus attention on the child victim, rather than on where the abuse took place, or who the victimiser was. It would incorporate the issue of informed consent and the child's ability to recognise the seriousness of what was happening.

In a society that truly cared for its children, we would agree that the issue is not who is abusing or where, but that children everywhere are in danger from sexual assault by adults. We would act swiftly to protect that child, and to curb the activities of the abuser. And we would then offer support and protection, where appropriate, to the rest of the victim's family.

Unfortunately, most of the definitions used today concentrate on the degree of kinship between the child and the abuser. A societal acknowledgement of the fact that it is not families who sexually abuse, but adult men and adolescent boys, would not only enable the abused child to receive the necessary protection, but would also facilitate the early establishment of appropriate therapy facilities for those who have chosen to exploit the most powerless members of our society: children.

Children lack the emotional, cognitive or maturational development to recognise that what the adult is doing is wrong. Because of their relative innocence in this area, the child's informed consent to such activities is never present. Despite the protestations of many abusers that the victims agreed to the sexual activities, for such consent truly to be present, two conditions would have to prevail:

1. The child would have to have informed knowledge of what s/he is consenting to.
2. The child would have to have the freedom and ability to say yes or no to an adult, whom they may know, love and trust, or indeed to any adult.

Everything that follows in this book is based on the definition of sexual abuse as being the involvement of children and young people in sexual activities which are intended to gratify adult sexual desires.

What happens when a child is sexually abused?

Child rape, or penetration of the child's vagina by a penis or other object, is only one of the wide spectrum of sexual abuses to which young children are being subjected. Because the law on incest demands evidence of such penetration as proof that a "crime" has been committed, it is extremely difficult to get a conviction in court. Similar difficulties apply for other forms of sexual abuse, despite the fact that these are much more likely to have informed the child's experience.

Sexual activity between an adult and a child may range from exhibitionism at one end of the spectrum, to full intercourse at the other.

Below is a range of sexually abusive practices, which have been identified by children and adult survivors, doctors, psychologists and social workers. Some of them may be familiar to you, others you may never have associated with child sexual abuse. All of them form part of the wide range of sexual abuses from which children may suffer long-term effects.

- Certain forms of nudity such as when an adult insists on parading around the home nude, or insists on watching the child bathe.

- Making the child watch while the adult undresses, or insisting that the child undresses in front of the adult.

This usually takes place when child and adult are alone.

- Genital exposure, when an adult exposes his or her genitals to the child, frequently inviting the child to touch or rub them.

- French kissing. This is a common form of abuse, and many children find it deeply distressing and confusing that what is normally an affectionate gesture on the part of an adult, in the form of a hug or a kiss on the head, or cheek, becomes such an unpleasant, intrusive experience.

- Masturbation by the adult, while making the child watch, or insisting that the child masturbates the adult, or that the adult masturbates the child. Another form of this is known as "dry" masturbation, when an adult rubs his penis against the buttocks of a small child.

- Oral sex: Mouth to genital contact, between adult and child.

- Fondling of the child's breasts or genitals. This sometimes takes place while the child is in the bath.

- Digital penetration, when the older person inserts a finger into the child's anus or vagina.

In the course of research into the problems of child sexual abuse, I asked victims what exactly happened to them. Some of them had experienced several types of molestation, others only one or two. However, it was apparent that they were all damaged in some way by what had happened to them, to a greater or lesser degree. Below is an analysis of their experiences.

Types of abuse	Number of abuses	Percentage of victims
Instrument used	5	11.9
Feeling of body	29	69.0
Penetration	17	40.5
Made to masturbate	27	64.3
Attempted intercourse	20	47.6
Genital Fondling	25	59.5
Mutual masturbation	12	28.6
Oral manipulation	25	59.5
Biting	14	33.3
Kissing (intimate)	21	50.0
Feeling of breasts	24	57.1
Use of pornography	13	31.0
Other abuses*	12	28.6
Total	244	581.0

The 42 victims included in the above table between them were subjected to 244 abuses. The average number of different types of abuse suffered by a victim was 6, though it ranged from 1 to 10.

* This category covered a range of abuses from indecent exposure to anal penetration and bestiality.

2 Myths and facts

"If we adults stop to think about what we are warning our children against, we become nervous, upset, guilty, and angry. It is not something we want to talk about. We hope that our vague warnings will be sufficient to keep our children frightened away from the unspeakable. The fact is, it has become a problem of staggering dimensions. Though only the tip of the iceberg has emerged, we find that sexual assault and abuse of children is a national epidemic. One in four girls is sexually assaulted before she reaches her eighteenth birthday, and recent evidence indicates that boys may be at equal risk. Experts agree that incest occurs in approximately one in ten families. Add to those startling figures all the children who are siblings or close friends of those who are victimized, all the children who never tell anyone that they have been abused, and all the children whose mothers are assaulted, and it

> amounts to one in two children directly or indirectly affected by sexual assault."
>
> Flora Colao and Tamar Hosansky,
> *Your Children should Know*

Despite the dramatic increase in public knowledge about the extent of child sexual abuse, we cling with tenacity to certain ill-founded beliefs. Behind this lies our reluctance to face the fact that any child, including our own, can become the victim of sexual assault and the perpetrator may be someone as loved and trustworthy as our partner, our sons, our brothers, our fathers, even our religious advisors. We cannot, and will not, believe that all our children are at risk as long as there is one person in the community who chooses to sexually abuse them. And when they tell us they are abused, we may resort to telling ourselves, and them, that they are imagining it all, that they shouldn't talk "about things like that", that it's bad to lie about adults.

Child sexual abuse can and does happen. The taboo is not against doing it, it is against talking about it. This taboo keeps the problem in the darkness of secrecy and thus encourages the very behaviour it is supposed to prevent.

The myths listed below are some of the most tenaciously held by all of us. Not to confront them is to continue to place our children in danger.

MYTH: **It won't happen to my children, I watch them all the time**

FACT: Child sexual abuse can and does happen. Contrary to popular myth, it is not taboo. However, talking about it has been taboo until recently.

Research findings show that 1 in 4 girls and 1 in 12 boys will probably be sexually assaulted before they reach the age of 16. In Dublin alone there will be approximately 850 new cases each year.

MYTH: **Children are usually assaulted by strangers**
FACT: About 95% of children are abused by someone who is known, trusted and/or loved by them. The abuse can take place either in the family home, or outside the immediate family (by uncle, grandfather, cousin, etc). ''Stranger danger'', while it exists, is not the only problem where protecting children is concerned.

MYTH: **Children tell lies about sexual abuse**
FACT: Children do not have explicit sexual knowledge to enable them to talk about this form of sexual activity, unless they have experienced it.

MYTH: **Sexual abuse rarely involves violent physical assault, so it's not really harmful**
FACT: To be a child is to be completely without power. If you are powerless then you have to depend on those around you for protection, for love, for your very survival. If one amongst that group around you chooses to exploit your powerlessness, you are filled with anger, which you may turn inwards, to develop into chronic depression, or outwards, manifesting as violence and hatred against society in general, and, in a renewal of the cycle of abuse, against children in particular.

Factors such as the closeness of the child's relationship with the abuser, the length of time the molestation continued and the age of the child will all contribute to the child's trauma and subsequent long-term effects.

Sexually abused children are:

1. Denied a childhood
2. Exploited and betrayed by a trusted person.

***MYTH:* It is better not to talk about the sexual abuse, the child will soon forget**

FACT: We now have the testimony of thousands of adults who were molested in childhood, and their message is loud and clear. Please, when your child wants to talk about what has happened, do not deny her/him. Listen, comfort, and reassure. To deny this will result in your child feeling that you do not care about what has happened, that you blame them in some way. Talking to a child when the need arises can be therapeutic both for the child and the parents, and it gives a chance to reassure the child that whatever the circumstances surrounding the abuse, s/he is in no way to blame for what has happened.

***MYTH:* S/he must have done something to provoke it**

FACT: This myth has been around for a long time and has meant that the victim has been blamed for something over which s/he had no control. Victims of sexual abuse can never be held responsible for what has happened to them, regardless of the circumstances. The blame lies with the offender. The *National Now Times* in 1982 reported a remark by a Wisconsin judge that a five-year-old rape victim was an ''unusually sexually permissive young lady''.

The *Irish Times* in 1986 reported a remark by a judge hearing a rape case where a 63-year-old woman was raped by a 24-year-old man, that it "wasn't a particularly bad case of rape since the victim had made a good recovery and did not require a doctor". The psychiatrist giving evidence on behalf of the accused stated that "he (rapist) was probably not responsible for his actions."

MYTH: **What they don't know can't hurt them**

FACT: Children need, and have the right to, information about the world they live in if they are to grow up in safety, with confidence, dignity and self-esteem.

MYTH: **Men who sexually abuse were themselves victims in childhood**

FACT: This reason is frequently quoted to justify a rapist's or child molester's behaviour.

While it is important to acknowledge that each of us carries a reservoir of forgotten experiences which inevitably have a bearing on our adult behaviour, this does not absolve us from accountability for our personal choices.

The facts as we know them are that many, many more female children than males are abused in childhood, yet there is no evidence that women sexually abuse children in great numbers in adulthood.

3 Who are the abusers?

> "We are still learning the many ways sexual abuse can occur. From fathers to babysitters, from teachers to clergy, there appears to be no end to the permutations children encounter in their efforts to negotiate the often predatory world of adults and older children."
>
> Sandra Butler,
> *Preventing Child Sexual Abuse*

Research and surveys carried out in different countries conclude that up to 1 in 4 girls and up to 1 in 12 boys can expect to be sexually abused before the age of 16. According to research carried out by MRBI (1987) for the Sanctuary Trust and the *Today Tonight* television programme, in Dublin there will be up to 850 *new* cases each year; at any one time there are up to 5000 children being sexually abused in that city. This does not indicate that 1 in 4 men are sexually abusing, but that those who are can frequently be abusing up to 10 children both inside and outside their homes, over a long period of time, often years. Many convicted abusers have admitted molesting "countless" children. When asked why they did it, they have said it was because they were not caught, or because no child ever said no.

Learning to sexually abuse

Despite the known figures for the numbers of children who have been sexually abused in the past, and estimated figures for those who will be in the future, it is not easy for a man to deliberately set out to molest young children or adolescents. The disapproval of society towards such behaviour acts as a considerable deterrent, and in addition there are internal and external "inhibitors" which have to be overcome.

According to researcher and clinical practitioner David Finkelhor (in Diana Russell, *Sexual Exploitation),* for sexual abuse to occur there must exist four preconditions:

a) The adult must have sexual feeling towards the child, or for children in general.
b) The adult must overcome his or her internal inhibitions against acting out sexual feelings.
c) The adult must overcome the external obstacles to acting out the sexual feelings.
d) The adult must overcome the resistance or attempts at avoidance by the child, if these occur.

Unless preconditions a) and b) exist, then c) and d) will be irrelevant. Where a), b) and c) occur, the child at risk may resist directly (by running away, for example), or indirectly (by being assertive in such a way as to avoid the sexual abuse). The child may not resist, and will then be victimised, or the child may resist but be overcome by force.

Child pornography and child sexual abuse

> " . . . these magazines gave me something to go by . . . on where things are, how they're done, and how it feels . . . (they) interest me and I enjoy reading them and learning new things about sex . . ."
>
> Teenage offender's comment about *Playboy*, reported in Summer 1986 edition of *Preventing Sexual Abuse*

Studies show that constant exposure to magazines and videos which relentlessly portray degrading images of women and children lowers resistance to becoming a victimiser, by eroticising sexual contact with children. There is a strong, well-argued case against censorship, but the line has to be drawn when lack of censorship involves the exploitation of a large and powerless section of the community.

Images of children in pornographic magazines

In a study funded by the US Department of Justice, entitled "Children, Crime and Violence in the Pictorial Imagery of *Playboy, Penthouse* and *Hustler*", the visual images of children in sexual and violent contexts were analysed in 683 issues, beginning with *Playboy's* initial December 1953 issue, up to *Playboy, Penthouse and Hustler* issues of December 1984.

The study identified three basic themes: non-sexual, non-violent activities, such as simple memories; violent activities such as murder, maiming or surgical procedures; and sexual activities such as intercourse or a child appearing nude.

A total of 6,004 photographs, illustrations and cartoons depicting children appeared in the 683 issues, with *Hustler* depicting children in one of the forms listed above an average of 14.1 times per issue. These images were interspersed with 15,000 images of crime and violence, 35,000 showing female breasts and 9,000 female genitalia.

Other findings included the following:

- 1,675 child images were associated with nudity.
- 1,225 child images were associated with genital activity.
- 989 child images were associated sexually with adults.
- 792 adults were portrayed as pseudo-children.
- 592 child images were associated with force.
- 267 child images were associated with sex with animals or objects.
- 51% of the child cartoons and 46% of the child photographs showed children between the ages of 3 and 11.
- More girls than boys were associated with sexual assault.
- More boys that girls were associated with violent assault.
- Almost all depictions of child sexual abuse portrayed the child as unharmed or as having benefited by the activity.

Reported by Dr Judith Reisman, President of the Institute for Media Education, 1986.

In the United States *Playboy* reaches 15,584,000 people per issue, *Penthouse* 7,673,000 and *Hustler* 4,303,000. All three magazines are obtainable in the UK and Ireland if you know where to look.

Using an "alcohol problem" as exoneration

> "I feel bad about it. I can't justify what I've done. I have never done anything like this before in my life, and I never dreamt I was capable of doing anything like this. I will never drink again. I know that."
>
> 31-year-old man, married with 3 children, to judge, after being found guilty of repeatedly sexually abusing a 10-year-old boy. He received a 5-year jail sentence. *(Irish Times,* March 1987)

The use and abuse of alcohol remains the most consistent excuse and justification used by offenders, their lawyers, psychiatrists and judges to exonerate them from culpability for sexually abusing a child. I scanned the pages of the *Irish Times* for the first 7 months of 1987, and below I give examples of how the "alcohol problem" excuse is presented to and accepted by judges. Had I turned to any other paper either in Ireland or the UK I would have found the same sort of depressing reports, about other children in other places, sometimes under more garish headlines, sometimes in more detail.

In June 1987 in the Dublin District Court, a 53-year-old father of 3 children pleaded guilty to sexual abuse of a child, but blamed a chronic alcohol problem. On hearing that he had two previous convictions, one for a similar offence in Chester, England in 1975, the judge commented, "You have pleaded guilty to one of the most serious and heinous charges". He then imposed a 12-month suspended sentence, on condition that the defendant stayed out of trouble for 5 years, continued his treatment for alcoholism at a treatment centre and never again approached or molested the young girl victim. (*Irish Times* 19/6/87)

In July 1987, after a policeman expressed fears in court that a sexual offender was receiving treatment only for an alcohol problem and not for his admitted sexual abuse of an 8-year-old girl, the judge commented that "it appears that if the alcoholism problem was solved the deviancy would be kept under cover." The offender had told his victim that if she ever told anyone he would batter her. (*Irish Times* 28/7/87)

Such a profound lack of understanding by the judiciary gives rise to serious questions about their competence to deal with sexual crimes against children, without their first undergoing some form of education and training in the whole area. It is not good enough to trot out some excuses and make the same generalisations about the offender when dealing with such contrasting issues as the sexual abuse of a child and the lack of a car insurance.

Becoming addicted

Once sexual molestation of a child has begun, the picture becomes bleak, not only for that child but for other children that the victimiser has access to, whether in the home, at work, or simply playing in the street.

Sexual abuse quickly becomes an addiction: it is perceived as a readily available, uncritical source of sexual pleasure, with a person who is unable to fight back physically, emotionally or psychologically. The victim's silence is obtained through a series of threats, bribes and blackmail. This inability by the child to resist is then interpreted by the abuser as "consent".

The victimiser becomes highly skilled, not only in self-deception, but also in keeping up a good public image. He is fully aware that what he is doing is unacceptable and wrong (otherwise why go to such lengths to enforce the victim's silence?). In order to overcome any feelings of guilt which he may have he devises a complex web of self-justifications to sustain him. Indeed, he frequently produces these in court, before a judge and jury, and so convincing is he that they too believe him and often ironically "convict" the victim.

Justifications for sexual abuse

- Men (like me) naturally need a lot of sex. I can't be expected to wait while my wife is in hospital.
- Everyone knows that men lose control when they're drunk. I wouldn't do it normally.
- I mean, you don't expect blokes to do the ironing and cooking and cleaning if the wife's out at work; your daughter should do it, shouldn't she?
- Daughters should do what they are told by their fathers, you expect that.
- Blokes get led on by women, it's not fair, it happens all the time.
- They pretend they don't like it, they act virtuous, but they love it really.
- Flaunting herself at me all the time like that, she's asking for it; besides she must be a bad girl if she goes on doing it.

- At least she's under my control, not messing about at all hours of the night with boys and getting into trouble with them. I'm not having that.

  Sarah Nelson, *Incest: Fact and Myth*

Back to the old routine

Unless clear-cut and unequivocal policies are instituted to protect the rights of the child which enable her/him to grow up in safety and peace at home, the mother is likely to be left without her child or children, without support, overwhelmed with feelings of guilt, inadequacy and powerlessness. And, the final irony, she frequently remains living with this man who has destroyed her and her family. To survive, she shuts up and puts up. His behaviour completely vindicated by the system, the child sexual abuser revives his addiction confident in the knowledge that everything now is OK: society knows and understands that he can't help himself.

The sexual abuser's personality

It is expected by many people that anyone who could sexually abuse a child must look, or talk, or behave differently from the rest of the community. There is always a profound sense of "who would have believed it?" when we find it is the man next door, or the priest or the lawyer, or our own beloved partner.

In November 1984 the NSPCC South-West Region Working Party produced a discussion paper, entitled "Developing a Child-Centred Response to Sexual Abuse". In a section headed "Father's characteristics where there may be a propensity to abuse", they identified some of the personality traits commonly found in abusers, particularly those abusing their own children, as follows:

- Rigid and authoritarian with family
- Ineffectual, with low self-esteem
- Poor ability to define relationship boundaries
- Fearful of discussing certain issues such as family sleeping arrangements or sexuality
- Excessive interest in pornography

4 Taking steps

> "A great deal of work must be undertaken to bring about the changes necessary to begin to solve the ubiquitous, painful and destructive problem of sexual exploitation. The first step is to realise the importance of this. The second step is to do it."
>
> Diana Russell, *Sexual Exploitation*

When to begin?

Although children as young as 1 year old have been sexually abused, studies show that around 5 years of age appears to be the time when most victimisation begins. We should bear in mind that this may be the earliest age when children are able to articulate in a comprehensive way what they are suffering. It is therefore sensible for parents to begin talking about safety well before this age.

However, as parents you may feel uncertain about where to begin. You may be worried about saying the wrong things and frightening or confusing the child. Will talking about assault warp the child's view of good sexual experiences when they grow up, or will they grow up thinking all sex is exploitative and bad? What about the child's natural sexuality? And, if you start teaching children that they can say no, and that they have rights over who touches them and how they are spoken to, will there be anarchy in the home? You may feel that talking to them about good, bad and confusing touch will inhibit you from hugging them freely. If they want to sit on your knee and give you a cuddle, should you let them? What if they have a nightmare and want to get into your bed for comforting? Will they become afraid of normal loving touch? Will you? Will they become suspicious and afraid of babysitters, uncles, neighbours and friends?'

How can you teach your children to trust, when the problem is that they already trust too much?

The rule of optimism

Concerns such as these have frequently had the result of preventing many parents from even making a beginning. Instead, they have adopted the rule of optimism: that "it" probably won't happen to their child but if "it" does happen, the child will tell because they tell you every little thing anyway.

Where sexual abuse is concerned, this is simply not the case. The child's silence is usually skilfully maintained by the abuser through threats, bribes and, frequently, the fear that you will not believe them. Indeed, optimism is a very poor defence against the determined victimser of children. By hiding behind such a strategy, you are placing your children at risk.

If we are to protect our children from the range of abusive experiences they may be exposed to while growing up, from school bullying to flashers, from teachers who use sarcasm as a classroom discipline to possible sexual or physical assault by someone known or unknown to them, we have to arm them (and ourselves) with the truth about their rights and those who would deny or remove them.

Preventive education teaches valuable lessons in assertiveness and communication. In fact, through preventive education, we are teaching children to trust themselves. And in time they will be grateful that you loved them enough to give them this trust.

Child's bill of personal safety rights

1. The right to trust one's instincts and feelings
2. The right to privacy
3. The right to say no to unwanted touch or affection
4. The right to question adult authority and say no to adult demands and requests
5. The right to lie and not answer questions
6. The right to refuse gifts
7. The right to be rude and unhelpful
8. The right to run, scream and make a scene
9. The right to bite, hit or kick
10. The right to ask for help

Flora Colao and Tamar Hosansky,
Your Children Should Know

The rights of children

In November 1959 the General Assembly of the United Nations approved The Declaration of the Rights of the Child. These included the provisions that all children have equal rights (Article 1),that they have the right to special protection for full physical, mental and social development (Article 2), the right to affection, love and understanding (Article 6) and the right to be protected against neglect, cruelty and exploitation (Article 9).

Do you think your child should have personal rights? Even when these rights might interfere with your family beliefs about rearing children, about discipline, about toeing the line, about doing what you say, no questions asked?

Insisting that your child obeys you, without question, without consultation about the rules you are imposing, can expose them to quite serious danger. If they have broken one of your house rules, they may feel unable to seek your help.

Children should not have to live in fear of breaking rules. They should be involved from the outset, if possible and practicable, in setting personal behaviour limits within and outside the home, knowing that if there is a lapse this can be discussed and dealt with in a reasonable manner.

Nobody's perfect. It's a cliché, but very often, in our anxiety to raise our children "properly", we insist that *they* are, and we sometimes punish them severely for even minor lapses.

If you study the "Child's Bill of Personal Safety Rights", you may feel a sense of hostility at what it advocates. However, closer inspection reveals that these are almost exactly the same "rights" which we, as adults, take very much for granted. So why do we feel it's not quite "right" for our children to assume the same rights?

The truth is probably that we spend much of their lives telling them that they should never question adult authority, that to refuse gifts is bad manners and shows ingratitude, that being rude and unhelpful may mean they will risk punishment, that they should never say no to a kiss even if the don't want it, in case they upset the person giving the kiss, that they should obey our commands without question, that these rules are "for your own good". Yet, it is precisely these child-rearing practices, which we have clung to as a model for "bringing them up well", which are placing children at risk!

The importance of repetition

Teaching something as complex as sexual abuse prevention cannot be achieved in one day. After all, we don't expect our children to learn to read in one day, or tie their shoe laces after one demonstration. It is an ongoing process throughout their childhood and adolescent years. It is this requirement which makes a home-based preventive education programme as important as a school-based one. Repetition is the key, at all ages. Your child will understand and absorb some safety strategies easily, but will take much longer over others. You cannot force information into their heads, if they are not psychologically ready to absorb it.

Language, listening and hearing

"One of the biggest areas of controversy has been and still is around explicitness. Many people do not want you to use explicit language. They want you to say 'private parts' or 'underneath your swimsuit'. I am very much opposed to that. I can understand people's concerns and we need to talk about them, but I want people to realise that when we don't say breast, penis, vulva, vagina, we are giving children a double message. What we are saying is, you can talk to me about sexual abuse, it's not your fault, there's nothing wrong with you. But your body is so bad that I can't even say what it is underneath your swimming suit."

Cordelia Anderson,
Preventing Child Sexual Abuse

Children do not have language explicit enough to tell you directly if someone is molesting them. They will say, "I don't like Uncle Dave tickling me", or "I'm not going to see Mr Smith's kittens again", or "I don't want Aunt Mary to kiss me goodnight." There may well be good reasons for any of these statements: Uncle Dave tickles long beyond the time when it's fun and enjoyable; Mr Smith has bad breath, and uses language which the child thinks is not nice; Aunt Mary insists on kissing directly on the mouth.

Remember, too, that a young child will perhaps think that you know why they want to restrain an older person from touching them, and they will assume you understand. This makes it doubly important for you to enquire gently into the reason for the child's discomfort.

Allowing your child to limit touch

We should always try to support the child's right to limit adults' behaviour with her/him. If necessary, we can ask

Uncle Dave not to tickle, or else support the child when s/he asks directly. Aunt Mary can be deflected in a nice way, or the child can practise saying, "Aunt Mary, I don't want to kiss you on the mouth, can I kiss your cheek?" If you support your children in making simple choices like these, where non-assaultive behaviour is involved, it will give the child confidence in her/his right to limit the behaviour of a possible molester, knowing that your support can be counted on.

Tina and Jane, two young sisters, insisted that they had told their parents that John, the babysitter, was abusing them. But the significant factor was their use of language: what they felt they were saying was not what their parents were hearing.

John kept "tickling" them and the little girls didn't like it and so asked their parents to tell him to stop. The parents asked John not to tickle the children so much as it made them too excited to sleep. The tragedy is that John, at 13 years old, had been seriously abusing both sisters for 2 years, but their limited language meant they could not ask for explicit help. They thought they had told their parents what was happening to them, and both children were very angry at them for not understanding and protecting them.

The need for balance

The balance to be achieved, when talking to young children about personal safety, is in making them aware without destroying their trust in adults.

Young children are likely to view *all* adults as godlike. It is important to remember that, although they are in the process of growing and changing, they still believe adults are right, even when the adult is doing something unpleasant or uncomfortable to them. Children need to be able to trust adults and feel secure in their care. The notion that adults can be untrustworthy, and may even hurt children, is disturbing and potentially frightening to them.

Already afraid of monsters, ghosts and other scary things, the young child may be terrified at the thought of yet another danger in her/his young life. So try to keep injunctions to "take care!" in the context of daily, friendly talks, giving plenty of hugs and kisses along the way. It is important to keep in mind that it is not only how often you speak to your child about keeping safe that matters but also the way you spell out exactly what the dangers may be.

The importance of language

Many parents feel frustrated that their child was molested despite telling them again and again to avoid talking to people. They believed that implicit in that message was information about sexual abuse. In fact, what their child probably heard was a warning about kidnapping! Somewhere in the grey areas between what the parents were saying and what the child was hearing lay all the dangers they were so concerned about.

The use of age-appropriate language is something each parent must decide about. Children all use language in different ways, and only you as a parent can decide what is the best approach for your individual child, altering your words if you see the child is having problems understanding you.

5 Safety and the pre-school child

> "Children trust or mistrust adults for reasons which often have nothing to do with how trustworthy that person is. They may be afraid of someone because he looks different and trust someone because he gives treats. Children who know what to watch for and know that they can tell someone are going to be more protected, not less."
>
> C. Adams & J. Fay,
> *No More Secrets*

You probably already spend a considerable time each day talking, reading and playing with your young child, and you may have begun incorporating simple safety techniques such as the way to cross the road, and warnings about the dangers of traffic.

When talking to your child use age-appropriate language and discuss safety issues in a calm, non-threatening tone of voice.

Avoid "scare tactics" to impress your child about the world outside the home. Young children need to make sense for themselves out of the generalisations they hear around them. Talking about bogeymen and "bad" men

is counter-productive and may well have the effect of creating a great fear of all men in the child.
Since most children are sexually abused by someone they know and trust, the aim is to make them aware enough to talk to you about anything that may make them uncomfortable and upset, rather than focusing on a particular type of person.

The approach should always be positive (play a game out of saying no politely, and saying no in an assertive way) rather than negative ("keep away from strangers, they may kidnap you", etc).

There are a number of safety strategies which you can adopt with your young child:

1. Teach your child her/his name and address.

2. If you have a telephone, show them how to answer it, without announcing the telephone number.

3. Have a trusted neighbour to whom your child can turn for help should you not be immediately available. Explain to your neighbour what you and your child are doing, in the presence of the child.

4. If your chosen neighbour has a telephone, teach your child that telephone number, and let him/her practise using it. Come to an arrangement with your neighbour whereby if they do receive a call from your child they will always check it out.

5. Give your neighbour a spare key, in case there is an accident in your home and the child is not tall enough to answer the door.

6. Tell your child that you must always know where they are if they go out to play, and, if they are moving from the immediate vicinity of your home, they should tell you where they are going. It's difficult for young children to remember this rule, so reinforce it each time s/he goes out to play, in a matter of fact way, saying "Now, what are you going to do?"

Body language

Teach your child that their body is their very own, and name the different parts of their bodies with them. Ideally, you should use the proper names, penis, navel, breasts, etc., just as you say nose, eyes, mouth, ears. If you have difficulty using these words stand in front of a mirror and repeat them to yourself. Remember, if there's any awkwardness it's on your own part; to your child they are just mere words!

Tell your child that their body is their own and that no one can touch it if s/he doesn't want them to.

Respect your child's right to privacy, if they show a desire for it. Young children may decide thay want to go to the lavatory "all by myself". If they want to close the door, let them. (You can avoid them being locked in by removing the key, or taking other appropriate steps).

Let your child say no to you, or other adults, without making them feel they are doing wrong. It is fundamental to the safety of all children that they have permission to say no, when they feel they need to.

Support your children

- Pay careful attention to who is around your children (unwanted touch may come from someone we like and trust).

- Back up your child's right to say "No".

- Encourage communication by taking seriously what your children say.

- Take a second look at signals of potential danger.

- Refuse to leave your children in the company of those you do not trust.

- Include information about sexual assault when teaching about safety, giving specific definitions and examples.

- Remind your children that even "nice" people sometimes do mean things.

- Prepare your children to deal with bribes and threats, as well as possible physical force.

- Urge your children to tell you about anyone who causes them to be uncomfortable.

- Virtually eliminate secrets between you and your children.

- Teach your children how to say "No", how to ask for help and to control who touches them, and how.

- Model self-protecting and limit-setting behaviour for your children.

C. Adams & J. Fay,
No More Secrets: Protecting Your Child from Sexual Abuse

Sharing secrets

Talk to your child about not keeping any secrets from you, even ones which Daddy or brother John or your babysitter may tell them. Encourage them, on a daily basis, to share any secrets they have been told. Actively discourage the use of secrets at this age. Later, when they are older, you can talk about the difference between secrets and surprises.

Let your children know that s/he can always come to talk to you if something is worrying them. Maybe a friend won't share toys, or maybe something they see on television is frightening them and needs explanation. Give them time to express their fears, and reassure them that you are there to listen, discuss and help. You can make subtle suggestions, but avoid instant solutions to all their worries. Instead, let them come up with ways of resolving things. This way they will learn to make choices for themselves at a young age.

Expressing feelings

Let your child show anger. Let them jump up and down with rage, or roll about the floor screaming. If we refuse to allow our children to express their feelings they will learn that they are not important, and this will act as a powerful inhibitor to future communication with us. They must learn that we care if they are feeling confused or unhappy or angry, and that we want to understand and help them.

Make a habit of hugging your children, kissing them hello, goodbye and goodnight. Make them feel loved, wanted and important to you. Don't assume they know these things.

Choosing a babysitter

Whether you choose a male or female babysitter, you need to have certain ground rules established before leaving your child in her/his care. Tell your child what the rules are, and repeat them to the babysitter in front of the child. If your child is due for a bath that night, then it should be completed before the arrival of the babysitter, so that you can say something like: "Mary has had her bath and she always puts her pyjamas on herself. She won't need any help with them. She goes to bed at 8.30, and is not to stay up later than that for any reason."

This strategy minimises the possibility of abuse resulting from the sitter bathing the child, or undressing her/him, or allowing her/him to stay up late as a bribe for playing a secret game.

Be alert to how your child reacts when you say a particular babysitter is coming. If your child seems nervous or unhappy about a particular person, you should ask if they want a different sitter. Don't just assume that your child is unhappy because you are going out.

Being on the alert

Only very rarely are there physical symptoms of sexual abuse in the very young child. Bruising around the vagina or anus, or sexually transmitted disease or a continuous vaginal discharge may alert you. In general, though, abuse in this age group is detected by observation, and by an awareness that something is distressing your child. A direct question such as "What's wrong with you?" will be unlikely to elicit any information, since the child may be unaware that anything is "wrong". However, some sensitive probing about secrets, or people they like/do not like or games they play with friends and grown-ups or the babysitter's behaviour, may be more successful in establishing the source of their distress. Their anxiety may have nothing whatever to do with sexual abuse, but nevertheless your child will need your support and help in these cases.

Language signals

Your child may be trying to draw your attention to the problems s/he is encountering by throwing out certain "messages" indirectly, such as:

- My bottom hurts
- My tummy hurts
- I have a secret
- I know a bad man
- Don't leave me here when you go out
- I'm not going to Mr Brown's house again

- I don't want to go to school

- I don't like you and Daddy going out

- Will I be put in prison?

- Will Daddy (uncle, grandad etc) go to prison?

- I don't like my bed/want to go to bed

- It hurts when I go to the toilet

Signs and symptoms

The appearance of any of the following signs or symptoms in your child should not throw you into a fit of panic. Their presence is an indicator that something is wrong, and you should take your child for a check-up, either with your family doctor, or at a children's hospital. Tell the person carrying out the investigation that you are worried about the possibility of sexual abuse (even if you have not the slightest idea who could be abusing). If abuse is ruled out and the symptoms persist, you should consider taking the child to another children's hospital, and asking for a proper validation to be carried out. This involves talking to the child without you present, and should only be done by a properly trained person.

Physical

- Bruising or inflamation around the anus or vagina
- Genital bleeding
- Tears in the vagina or around the anus

- Warts in the anus
- Pain or itching in the genital area
- Vaginal discharge
- Recurrent sores around and inside mouth

Behaviour

- Overclinging
- Fearful of men/older people generally
- Compulsive masturbation
- Oversexualised behaviour
- Wetting and soiling bed
- "Frozen" watchfulness

6 Strategies for 7-12 year olds

> "You'd better not never tell nobody but God. It'd kill your mother."
>
> Alice Walker, *The Color Purple*

If you are starting prevention education with your child at this age, it is important that you first read Chapter 4, "Taking steps." Also many of the basic safety strategies for the pre-school children in the previous chapter equally apply now. I have built on them in this section, to take account of children's growing understanding of the world around them.

At this age, your child will be leaving you for the greater part of each day to go to school. Most young children look forward to spending time with their friends, revelling in learning to read and write, learning to make decisions for themselves about who to befriend, who to avoid, and having a measure of independence outside the home for the first time. During this time their moral values, already hesitantly formed, are strengthened, and they are frequently vocal about "right" and "wrong". Their ability to judge when something is wrong for them is acute, but they are often not sure whether feeling wrong about something gives them the right to take steps to prevent it.

Using the telephone

As well as showing your child how to use the telephone in the home (see previous chapter), teach them how to use the public telephone system. Give them plenty of opportunities to practise this so that they are quite familiar with the procedure. Make sure they memorise your telephone number and the numbers of one or two trusted people in case a crisis arises and you are not at home.

Playing outside the home

Teach your child three golden rules when playing outside the home, particularly if s/he is invited into someone else's home to play:

1. Do I want to go into this house?
2. Have I told my parents where I'm going?
3. Can I get help if I need to?

If the answer to any one of these questions is no, then your child should not go into anyone else's house. Practise asking the question every so often when your child is going outside to play with friends.

Make sure your child does not play in isolated places, local parks, empty houses, etc, even with friends.

Being collected at school

Teach your child a codeword which only you and s/he knows. Then if anyone turns up at school, even if it is someone the child knows well, saying that they have been asked to pick up your child, unless s/he uses the codeword the child can refuse to go with them. Remind your child of this plan at frequent intervals, putting yourself in the part of the "collector". Make your child understand that they must resist all pressure to go with the "collector" unless they are given the codeword.

Being followed

Tell your child that if s/he suspects that an older person is following them, they should go to the nearest shop, or similar public place, talk to a person in charge and ask to use the phone to call a trusted person to collect them.

If their suspicions are not taken seriously by the person whom they have asked for help, they should try to insist that they are afraid, and need help. If that fails, they should go to another shop, or ask an older person in the street to walk with them until the danger has passed.

Travelling in lifts

Lifts, which are confined spaces with only one escape route, are danger spots for everyone, but especially for children. It is a simple procedure for an abuser to follow an intended victim into a lift, press the "stop" button between floors, and carry out a sexual assault. A further risk occurs if a child enters a lift but is too small to reach the control panel.

If you know your child will be using a lift, show her/him how to use the controls, how to judge whether the lift is travelling upwards or downwards, and how to say "go ahead, I'm waiting for my mother/father" if s/he doesn't want to travel with somebody they don't like the look of. If your child is in the lift and someone enters that they feel uneasy about, they can press the appropriate button and get off at the next floor.

School route

Study your child's route to and from school, whether s/he travels alone, or with friends, and change the route regularly if possible. Make sure they always have enough money for a telephone call should a crisis arise. Expect them home at a certain hour, and always question them gently but firmly if they are late.

Play "what if" games

From an early age all children learn about the world around them through play. Teaching through play is a very effective strategy at all ages. Start with simple concepts like:

What if you come home from school and there's nobody here?
What if you need to phone home – show me how you phone?
What if someone you like is in bad trouble and wants you to keep it a secret?
What if the babysitter asks you to keep a secret?
What if someone you know puts their hands in your pants?
What if someone at school takes your bike, and wants you to do something you don't like before you can get it back?
What if Mr Smith (a neighbour) asks you if you want to go into his house to see his new puppies?
What if someone you have never seen before turns up outside school, calls you by your name, and says your mum has sent him/her to fetch you as she is ill?

Don't try to teach/role-play all these games at once. Take each "what if" and talk it through with your child, making sure that they have choices, and that they are comfortable with the final choice – it's their safety which these games are aimed at protecting, so it is important to make them feel confident about their choice.

Bribes

Many young children are tricked into sexual activities through the use of financial or other types of bribes. Faced with the opportunity of earning a little extra pocket money for comics, sweets or something being saved for, the child may willingly seize the opportunity offered, which may lead to such abuse as masturbating an abuser, or undressing in front of him.

To the child it may appear harmless enough, but unfortunately when s/he tries to stop the activity, the abuser frequently resorts to blackmail of the "I'll tell your parents what you were doing, and you'll get into trouble" type. This may be the first indication for the child that what s/he is doing is unacceptable to you, and in order not to bring trouble on themselves they may agree to continue the activities.

This "consent" by the child then becomes the open sesame for the abuser to expand the child's sexual involvement with him.

> **"The Court heard how the boy met the defendant when going on a message for his mother. The defendant stopped him and asked him if he wanted sweets and if he wanted to earn £5."**
>
> ***Irish Times* 4/5/87**

Teach your child never to take sweets, money or other treats from anyone without first checking with you. Reassure them that most of the time it will be OK, like when they get a birthday present of money, but that it is always safer to check.

Secrets versus surprises

> "One difficulty in dealing with child sexual abuse is that sometimes the victims experience physical pleasure. This compounds the confusion and makes the children feel that they are accomplices and that their bodies have betrayed them. An added problem may be that the abuser is also the only person from whom the child is receiving any type of affection, however inappropriate. This is particularly true if the abuser is a member of the child's family.
>
> By telling children that no touches, hugs or kisses should be kept secret, you are helping them to define the boundaries and giving them permission to seek an adult's help. Children may feel responsible or even guilty about what has happened and you must try to give them a way of telling in order to relieve that burden."
>
> Michele Elliot, *Keeping Safe*

Since many children are bound up in a web of secrecy by the abuser, it is important to talk with them about the difference between secrets and surprises. For example:

Surprises are for birthdays and Christmas when everyone wants to keep quiet about a present or a planned trip. They are enjoyable and fun and will not hurt anyone.

Secrets can make you feel very unhappy, and if they do, you have the right to ask someone about them.

If an older person does something to you, like touching you in a way that makes you feel a bit uncomfortable, and then tells you that it is a secret between the two of you, you should not feel you have to keep that secret. Some secrets are in fact bad to keep and it is always safer to check if you are unsure.

If your friend tells you something frightening or confusing is happening to them, but that it is a secret, and you are worried for your friend, then you have the right to check it out with a trusted adult.

Make it a rule that you never agree to keep a secret between you and any older person, even someone you know very well.

Define sexual assault

There is good touch, bad touch, and, most difficult of all, confusing touch. A hug by an older person, which yesterday made the child feel good, may be subtly altered today, and now the hug makes the child feel uneasy. For a child, this change in the quality of the touch can cause a good deal of confusion simply because it is so hard for her/him to define what exactly has changed, and why it makes them feel uncomfortable now.

If a hug is given tomorrow, and again there are subtle changes in it, then your child will probably receive it as no longer just confusing, but something s/he definitely doesn't like and wants to stop.

Ask your child what they would do if someone tried to touch them in a way which made them feel uncomfortable. Don't be surprised if, despite all your earlier discussions with them, they say, "I don't know"! It is frustrating, but it underlines my point in the earlier chapter that repetition is important.

If your child asks what you mean, exactly, then you can lead in by saying, "If anyone tried to touch your bottom or your penis, what would you do?" (If you still cannot use these words, then use the ones you are comfortable with).

Point out that no one, absolutely no one, should touch their body in a way that frightens or confuses them, and that they have the right to say no. In fact, they should tell the toucher that they will inform their parents immediately.

Tell your child that sometimes even people whom they know very well may try to touch them in this way, but that they should always say no in as firm a voice as possible, and then try to get away and tell someone.

Possibly someone older may ask them to touch their genitalia, or ask them to undress, or try to kiss them by putting a tongue in their mouth. Again, impress upon your child that nobody has the right to ask them to do this, and even if they are too frightened or confused to say no at the time, they should tell someone they trust as soon as possible.

Your child also has the right to say no to someone touching them in any way, for no other reason than that s/he just does not want that contact just then.

In every child's life, there is usually a certain amount of peer group playing of doctors and nurses, and mothers and fathers, when children will act out scenes from adult life around them. Don't confuse this play with other, inappropriate play.

However, if you feel that one of the group is playing in a sexually provocative or otherwise inappropriate way, be alert to other signs of stress in the child, and if you feel you need further advice, talk to the child's teacher, or, if appropriate, the child's parents about it. Avoid saying who you think the abuser may be: your concern is that their child may be in trouble. They may not welcome your worry, but it is better to do this than do nothing.

If you are really worried, telephone the social worker or public health nurse attatched to the school, or the doctor's surgery, and explain why you are concerned.

Assertiveness

Say No! like you mean it:	
Can I wear your watch?	NO!
Can I borrow your bike?	NO!
Give me that money!	NO!

You have already started teaching your child assertiveness when you give them permission to say no.

Identify some of the things which your child feels uneasy about, like a kiss from a whiskery uncle, which they can't control, and let them practise asking uncle not to kiss them like that as it makes them feel uncomfortable. It takes a bit of practice, and even courage (even adults often find asserting difficult), so do have patiece.

Encourage your child to have eyeball to eyeball contact with the person they are refusing, since that gives them personal space and intimidates the asker.

Another example of assertiveness is learning to say no when someone you really like wants a favour. How difficult it is to say no nicely! You and your child should practise asking each other favours, putting on the pressure bit by bit as your child becomes more confident.

Assertiveness, too, is the self-defence yell and it is great fun to teach: you should try to make it as blood-curdling as possible! Have your child or children sit around in a circle and shout/echo back words you say. You yell out a word (like NO!) or a sound (like a yell) and they shout it back at you. Being in a group helps them to yell loudly without feeling self-conscious. Some children may become frightened or upset at this procedure, but you should explain that these are normal feelings and they shouldn't feel ashamed or embarrassed about them. This exercise should be done frequently, to encourage your group to shout louder and longer. Get your child to practise it with you and with other friends, and tell them to use it if they are in a situation which they feel is going to endanger them.

The father of six-year-old Adam who was abducted and murdered said:

> ''Adam was a model child, he never went to the park by himself. He never disobeyed, never. I taught him to listen to adults, to respect his elders and to be a little gentleman. I never taught him how to scream. He might be alive if he had screamed.''
>
> From Michele Elliot, *Keeping Safe*

Rules which may place your child in danger

We all have family rules, guidelines by which we learn to live with one another, and become sociable human beings. However, if we are to keep our children safe, we have to give them permission to break these rules. Indeed we should re-examine all our family rules to see if any of them might need to be revised. I am thinking particularly of the following examples:

1. Don't be rude. If someone speaks to you, you should answer.

2. Be nice to people. It's not nice to hurt people's feelings.

3. You are responsible for taking care of other people.

Use these family rules as a basis for your revision and add to them with examples from family rules which apply in your home. Remember that such restrictions actually limit your child's ability to react assertively in certain situations. Look back at the ''Child's Bill of Rights'' in Chapter 4: you may find some of your family rules hidden there!

When we are teaching our children to Take Care! we must make it absolutely clear to them that, when necessary, they have our full permission to break these rules.

The most important thing is that if they are in a situation which they feel may be dangerous, they can say no, they can run away, they can yell and they can tell someone and get help. In America this drill is known as ''No! Go! Yell! Tell!.

Tell your child that s/he has the right to say no. Even if s/he likes the person, it's OK to say no.

What your child is feeling is important

It is important that your child knows that what s/he feels about the adults in their life is of concern to you. Your child may be worried that s/he dislikes a particular uncle or cousin, and feel guilty about this. You can reassure her/him that it is not necessary to like everyone just because they are an adult or an adult relation.

If you ignore what your child is trying to tell you, s/he will probably decide that you don't really care about their feelings, and you lose the opportunity of helping them when they are fightened or confused about something that has taken place.

Make a habit of telling your child that s/he is important to you, and that you want to know if anything is worrying them.

Signs and symptoms

As this is a developmental range of signs and symptoms, you should also check the full list in Chapter Eight. The presence of any of these signs and symptoms is not necessarily a positive indication that your child is being sexually abused, but where one or more is detected, the cause should be investigated.

Physical

- Recurrent tummy pains
- Recurrent urinary infections
- Soiling and wetting the bed

Behaviour

- Persistent nightmares
- Reluctance to go to bed
- Hysterical fits
- Withdrawn from family and peer group
- Few or no friends of own age
- Provocative sexual behaviour
- Inappropriate sex play with dolls and peer group
- Excessive interest in video nasties and pornographic magazines
- Excessive use of sexual innuendo
- Fear of the dark
- Fear of adults
- Panic attacks
- May have more money than normal (bribes)
- Abrupt changes in moods, attitudes and behaviour
- Exaggerated need for attention and praise
- Over-anxious about the dark, being alone etc.
- Problems socialising at school
- Unable to stay awake at school
- Constant nightmares

Further reading

The Willow Street Kids by Michele Elliot. Highly recommended both for children to read alone and for parents to read and discuss with them.

It's OK to say No by R. Lenett & B. Crane.

No More Secrets For Me by Oralee Wachter.

7 Prevention tactics for the adolescent

> "Dear God,
> I am fourteen years old. I have always been a good girl. Maybe you can give me a sign letting me know what is happening to me!"
>
> Alice Walker, *The Color Purple*

Prevention education and adolescents

Whether they are aware of it or not, most adolescents will already have experienced numerous abusive incidents, such as bullying, sexual harassment in school, obscene telephone calls, being followed by a stranger, as well as dealing with peer-group pressure to look at video nasties or pornographic magazines.

Adolescence is a particularly crucial time since the transition from pre-teens to adulthood can be painfully stressful, even without the added worries of sexual assault.

In this period, many young people begin to develop personality traits which may eventually lead to their becoming a victim, or a victimiser, although the roots of these traits will have been laid down during childhood.

The communication gap

It is quite common for a communication gap to open up in an otherwise happy and comfortable parent/adolescent relationship, if one side or the other feels they are not being treated fairly. Expectations shift and change, and aspirations are not discussed fully. It is up to the parent to keep the lines of communication open at all times and thus to try to bridge the gap.

Getting the balance right

Balancing normal parental worries with the need to allow a growing freedom for our children can seem impossible. Added to this is parental confusion about what teenagers really know about life. How much misinformation have they taken in? Would they really tell if they got into trouble? Do they know when they are walking into danger?

Teenagers seem to "know it all". They go to extraordinary lengths to be "cool". They act adult one day and revert to infancy the next. They frequently lack self-esteem, take enormous risks, and see all issues in terms of black or white.

But if you probe a little into their real knowledge about sexual assault, pregnancy, good health, disease, or issues of public and private morality, you may find an abyss of ignorance.

It is the combination of seemingly sophisticated attitudes and actual ignorance which makes all adolescents vulnerable to exploitation.

They have misconceptions about what sexual assault

is and how and why it happens. If it happens to them, they may feel it's their fault, therefore tell no one or seek any help. They are unwilling to consider or discuss their own sexuality.

They are afraid to seek help or advice in case this is seen as an inability to run their own lives.

On the other hand, they are flooded with conflicting messages about sex and violence from radio, films, television, music, magazines and books.

The need to make personal choices

If their childhood has been one where they were raised according to rigid family rules they may now be unable to exercise choices in their decision-making about sex, risk-taking, using drugs, or drinking alcohol, since they frequently do not know what choices are available or how to go about making them, particularly under peer pressure. If they have been used from childhood to making their own decisions, it will be easier at this time to exercise choice.

Being assertive

A significant number of adolescents do not know how to say no, what they can say no to, who they can say it to or when, or what to do if no is not enough. The strategies used for teaching 7-12 year olds how to be assertive are even more important for this age group, as teenagers have more access to freedom and often bow down under pressure, fearful of seeming "different".

What is sexual exploitation?

In *Sexual Violence: The Unmentionable Sin,* M.M. Fortune

offers the following definitions of three types of material which your teenager will encounter:

Pornography: Sexually explicit material which portrays abuse, violence and degradation for the purpose of arousal and entertainment.

Erotica: Sexual materials which may or may not be sexually explicit and are used for the purpose of arousal and entertainment. Erotica does not include violence, abuse or degradation of a person.

Sexual education materials: Sexually explicit materials used for the purpose of education or therapy, which do not include violence, abuse or degradation.

What adolescents don't know about exploitation, sexual assault, and sexual harassment can hurt them. Their lack of information in these, and many other, areas leaves them vulnerable. Many of them desperately want to know more about these issues but are afraid or embarrassed to ask.

A possible way of introducing issues into normal, everyday conversation is to refer to a particular current issue, say a rape case, which is in the newspaper, or mention the fact that your local Rape Crisis Centre is looking for funds. A straightforward question such as, "Have any of your friends been raped or sexually assaulted?" or a comment on the case in the newspaper, will get the ball rolling.

Remember, whatever issue you are discussing, do not talk for more than five or six sentences unless your teenager encourages you: any longer and you will lose their attention, particularly if you are entering a previously unknown area. Also, don't use scare tactics to get them to listen. They will just tune you out. Teenagers want you to understand that they have full confidence that they can take care of themselves and that nothing bad will ever happen to them.

Consent versus force

Adolescents are likely to be confused about sexual behaviour: what is allowed, what they want, how they can set limits and still keep a boyfriend, what is consenting sex, and what isn't.

If you want to introduce the topic of consent as against force, then plan ahead. Reassure your teenager that you are not probing into her/his private life, but that you think it would be OK for you both (or indeed the whole family) to discuss the pros and cons of consent, or force, pornography, etc. Maybe the school has had a visit from the Rape Crisis Centre or a family planning clinic. Start by asking what went on, what was discussed, how the class felt about the visit.

Take one aspect at a time, and resolve not to use scare tactics. Remember to use the five-sentence rule. Anything you need to say can be said in five sentences. After that you are repeating yourself.

Listen to your child's answers. If they are vague, don't press for specifics, as you will sound like an interrogator. Don't be upset if your teenager isn't as riveted by the discussion as you are: s/he may be more interested in a date that evening! You will probably get a better response if the discussion takes place at a more convenient time, like during a shopping trip, or lunch together, or while making supper.

Different kinds of touch

Unless your teenager recognises and understands that touch can be confusing, or exploitive or violent, they may not know how to avoid some sexual assaults. Parents themselves are frequently confused about bodily touch with their growing children, and they become unsure about what kind of touch with them is appropriate. Also, because of the fear now engendered about incest, what should be normal touch is often suspect. Unfortunately some variations of touch, sympathetic touch or affectionate touch, can be interpreted differently because of these sexual overtones.

There are many different kinds of touch:

Friendly touch: playful punches, pats on back, rubbing of shoulders or arms.

Acquaintance touch: a handshake or a quick pat on arm between acquaintances who don't know each other well enough to hug comfortably when they meet.

Affectionate touch: an expression of affection between the giver and the receiver, such as a hug or squeeze of the arm.

Exploratory touch: gesture which explores the texture of material or skin.

Nurturing touch: a non-demanding, comfortable touch, like back rub or hair being brushed.

''Accidental'' touch: generally a sign of subtle harassment, such as when someone fleetingly touches your breast or rubs against you, apparently by accident.

Other examples of touch with which we are familiar are:

Sensual touch
Exploitive touch
Violent touch
Confusing touch
Sympathetic touch
Bad touch

Sex role expectations

We programme our children for adult life, either consciously or sub-consciously, through such things as language, clothes, education and training. This programming can have a different emphasis, depending on whether our child is male or female. Even if, as parents, we strive conscientiously to avoid sex-role stereotyping, we cannot control what influences prevail in the classroom, in the youth club, in the films they see, the books they read. At best, we can raise the issue of stereotyping at home, and discuss it with them, alerting them to the ways in which they may be left vulnerable and powerless by it.

Here are ideas for a discussion on sex roles with your children:

- Ways in which education for boys differs from that for girls.
- The jobs which men and women traditionally do.
- What makes a "real" man and a "real" woman? Do these exist?
- Should Home Economics teachers be
  Men?
  Women?
  It doesn't matter?
- Boys do better:
  in an all-boys school?

in a mixed school?
it makes no difference?

- Is it more important for a man to have a career than it is for a woman if:
  the woman wants to have a family?
  she already has a family?
  always?

- Women often earn less money than men because:
  they can't work as hard?
  they don't need the money so much?
  they don't get such well-paid jobs?

Conflicting Messages from Advertising

> "One of the media's worst aspects is its frequent linking of sex and violence. There are ads and rocks videos which feature women who are tied down, physically threatened, being hit. There are TV shows in which characters fall in love with those who raped them. On other TV shows, the sexy male and female detective team may shoot the "bad guy", and congratulate each other with a long kiss, standing over the body – gun still in hand. The media knows the two things that sell: sex and violence. What are kids learning? That violence is sexy? that sex usually involves violence?"
>
> C Adams, J Fay & Loreen-Martin,
> *NO is not enough*

What message do you think is contained in the "Impulse" (a body lotion) advertisement which states: "Men can't help acting on it?"

Do you think that dressing children to look like sexually provocative adults is a good way to promote cheese slices packaged as "Easi-Singles?" This particular advertisement combines the twin messages of sex and violence, using children.

Is it essential to the selling of soap that a young girl's bath towel has to fall off, revealing her nude, in a particularly offensive example of television advertising?

As parents, you can alert your children to what is degrading and exploitive on television. As a family, you can write a letter of complaint to the newspapers, to the television authority, to the Advertising Standards Authority. The important thing is to react!

What is rape?

Rape is the ultimate abuse of power, perpetrated through a violent sexual assault. It is committed by men, usually on women and young girls, but more and more frequently we hear of young boys and adult men also being raped by members of their own sex.

All the available knowledge on rape and rapists has been provided either by victims who have had the courage to seek help, or apprehended rapists. From research carried out with the latter, it is clear that many rapists have sex available to them through their girlfriends and wives. They do not therefore need normal sexual release. They see their victims not as human beings, but in terms of "cunts" or "whores". They identify their motivation to rape as being a need to feel powerful and dominant.

An extremely good and useful book which looks at the history of rape is now available. Written by Susan Brownmiller, it is entitled *Against Our Will*. It provides food for thought in every paragraph, and should form the basis for a number of thoughtful discussions in the home.

Your teenager and date rape

> "In the last nine months alone in the Dublin courts seven cases that could fall into the category of 'date rape' have been criminally prosecuted. In each of these seven cases the women involved said they were raped by men they met at discos, dances and nightclubs. They were men they liked initially and had danced with in the course of the evening – men they were getting to know. They were men who walked or drove them home at the end of the night. The women had encountered their alleged attackers in situations so far removed from their traditional image of a rapist that they were not aware of the dangers at the time. These were the men they trusted – in some cases to protect them from the 'dark stranger' rapist they feared."
>
> Noirin Hegarty, *Irish Times* 6/3/87

All the available studies show that teenagers are most vunerable to being raped by someone they know, frequently someone they are dating. Date rape (also called acquaintance rape) can happen in a car, in a friend's home, in your own home. Date rape and child sexual abuse are the two most common forms of teenage assault.

''When I was 16 I had a boyfriend who went to the same school as me. One night we had been to the local village dance and when we came back to my house he made me lie on the floor and forced oral sex on me. I kept saying no, but he threatened to 'nut' me if I didn't shut up. I knew my parents were upstairs in bed, but I was scared they would find out what was happening, so I kept quiet. My boyfriend was acting totally out of character and this scared me as well. He had never been violent to me before, but I knew by this stage he was quite capable of it, as he had had a few drinks. We had been having sex quite frequently up to this point, but it was just straightforward intercourse. I remember lying in bed that night feeling numb and blank. The next day I met him on the school bus as usual and the relationship carried on as normal.''

Adolescent talking to author, 1987

In date rape, teenagers get involved in verbal pressure to engage in sexual activities. Emotional blackmail is used (''don't you love me?'') as well as bribery (''If we do this I'll go to a film with you on Sunday'') and false expectations (''What did you think we were dating for? You must be frigid''). Usually the teenager agrees to sex, following this barrage of pressure. This is very different from consenting sex.

The difference between rape, sexual exploitation and consenting sex is the degree and the kind of pressure and force used.

Five prevention tactics for adolescents

1. Agree with your teenager the ground rules, so that s/he feels protected rather than restricted. You may not achieve instant agreement, but negotiations should continue in a non-aggressive atmosphere, involving the whole family, where appropriate.

2. If your teenager agrees to be home by a certain time, agree that s/he contacts you if a problem arises on any occasion when this agreement cannot be kept.

3. Have a fall-back plan with a friend or neighbour, so that your teenager can call them if an emergency arises and you are not available.

4. Agree a no-questions-asked policy. If a rule is broken, and your teenager finds her/himself in trouble, have a no-questions-asked strategy agreed. Fear of your anger when a rule is broken may prevent the request for help, and a rape or other sexual assault could ensue. The important thing is to provide a safety net to prevent tragedy. If you wish to pursue the rule-breaking, then bring up the subject the next day or so. You may find that your child brings it up first.

5. Where possible make sure that your teenager always has "panic money", so that there is always a way of bailing out of any situation and still getting home.

Role-play which helps to avoid victimisation

Many adults feel self-conscious about role-playing, but it's a good idea to encourage your teenager and a group of friends to do this with each other:

- Practise assertive responses to requests for sex.
- Practise making choices based on what you want. Not what someone else says you should want.
- Practise changing your mind, when your feelings change. Any situation, which at first seems OK, can change rapidly, and become very uncomfortable.
- If you feel you are being treated badly or unfairly, either at home, at school, at work, or by a friend, practise asserting your right to be treated differently. It may not seem worth the trouble, but being treated well should be one of your expectations.
- Take another action, when being assertive is not enough. Practise walking away from a situation, where you feel endangered.
- If there is the threat of physical violence in the air, leave the situation, asking other friends if they want to leave too. They may laugh at you and you may be afraid you'll get into trouble at home, but trust your feelings in these situations.

Signs and symptoms

Although childhood abuse may have ceased some years ago, the long-term effects may begin to manifest themselves during adolescence. If you are still unaware of the existence of sexual abuse, you may not make the connection between the present symptoms and the past experience, and neither will your teenager. If any of these signs and symptoms arise now, you should try to establish, through sympathetic questioning, if anything unpleasant has happened, in the past or more recently, to your child, that they would like to talk to you about. Be careful to give reassurance that your full support will be forthcoming, no matter what the problem is. Don't press too hard for information. Plant the seed that you are there to listen and help. The experience may have been repressed so successfully that it cannot be recalled at this time. Consider also the possibility that it may be something other than sexual abuse which is creating stress in the child's life.

Physical

- Pregnancy
- Sexually transmitted disease
- Self-mutilation
- Anorexia
- Bulimia

Behaviour

- Suicide attempts
- Running away
- Depression
- Under-achieving at school
- Over-achieving at school
- Truancy from school
- Without friends/social isolation
- Promiscuity
- Low self-esteem
- Pseudo-adult behaviour
- Homicidal rage attacks
- Drug, alcohol or other substance abuse

- Hysterical attacks
- Staying away from home as much as possible
- Refusal to bring friends home
- Poor concentration at school
- Wary of older person in house
- Compulsive washing of body
- Poor emotional control
- Chronic sense of personal injustice

Further reading

NO is not enough: Helping Teenagers Avoid Sexual Abuse by C. Adams, J. Fay and J. Loreen-Martin.

Parents and Teenagers by A. Lawton.

Too Close Encounters and What to Do About Them by Rosemary Stones.

8 Signs and symptoms

> "Children often feel that parents are all-powerful and have eyes in the back of their heads. Their natural conclusion therefore is that parents know and don't disapprove of what's going on. So a child who is being touched, kissed or hugged in any way they dislike feels powerless to stop it."
>
> C. Adams et al, *No More Secrets*

Traditionally children have been taken to the family doctor, or to a hospital, when they have shown signs of illness or great distress. Until very recently it was rare for sexual abuse to be diagnosed. Doctors were not trained to identify it, nor did they know what to look for.

In like manner, many children and adolescents have ended up in a psychiatrist's clinic for treatment for the symptoms of abuse, such as aggression, hostility, depression, or disruptive and anti-social behaviour. Unfortunately, the "cause" continues, and so the treatment of the symptoms cannot possibly be successful, and the patient is referred on to another clinic or specialist, in a pattern which often repeats itself throughout life. Many such victims have ended up as long-term inmates of mental institutions. Nobody asked them what had happened to them in childhood, and they, used to being locked into a conspiracy of silence, never betrayed the secret imposed on them in childhood.

Many of the following signs and symptoms can present at any time in childhood, with the exception of pregnancy. The presence and detection of one or more of the symptoms is primarily an indicator that something is wrong in the child's or young person's life. However, although it is difficult to face up to, we should always at least consider whether sexual abuse may be the cause, either within the home or else outside it.

"From the time she was 3 years old she has complained about pains in her tummy, pains in her hands, sore throats. Then she has been afraid of the dark for as long as I can remember: she would start to scream as soon as the light went out at night. He was always the one who took her to the doctor, and who insisted on staying with her to comfort her. I just couldn't understand it when she stopped talking or smiling – all the others are so good-natured. I put it down to her being jealous of them, her being the eldest. Over the years from when she was 3 until she was 10 we went to the doctor at least once a month. He sent us to all the children's hospitals, and they sent us to a child guidance clinic. Then she told her teacher.

How can the child ever forgive me for not realising? Why didn't some of these doctors realise? I can't sleep at night for worry about her but at least she talks to me now, and I've told her I just didn't know what was going on and am terribly sorry. I don't know, do you think we will ever be right?''

Mother whose husband abused her eldest child. She has now found out that he was also abusing all her other children (Dublin 1985).

The list below is a progressive range of symptoms. Many of those presenting in the adolescent stage will not be found in the pre-school child, whereas those showing in the pre-school child can be present also at an older age. You will also find these signs and symptoms in the appropriate chapters, as a reminder of what to look for.

PRE-SCHOOL

Physical

- Bruising or inflamation around the anus or vagina
- Genital bleeding
- Tears in the vagina or around the anus
- Warts in the anus
- Pain or itching in the genital area
- Vaginal discharge
- Recurrent sores around and inside mouth

Behaviour

- Overclinging
- Fearful of men or adults generally

- Compulsive masturbation
- Over-sexualised behaviour
- Wetting and soiling bed
- "Frozen" watchfulness

7-12 YEAR OLDS

Physical

- Recurrent tummy pains
- Recurrent urinary infections

Behaviour

- Soiling or wetting the bed
- Persistent nightmares
- Reluctance to go to bed
- Hysterical fits
- Withdrawn from family and peer group
- Few or no friends of own age
- Provocative sexual behaviour
- Inappropriate sex play with dolls and peer groups
- Excessive interest in video nasties and pornographic magazines
- Excessive use of sexual innuendo
- Fear of the dark
- Fear of adults
- Panic attacks
- Having more money than normal (bribes)
- Abrupt changes in moods, attitudes and behaviour
- Exaggerated need for attention and praise
- Over-anxious about the dark, being alone, etc.
- Problems socialising at school
- Unable to stay awake at school
- Constant nightmares

Physical

- Pregnancy
- Sexually transmitted disease
- Self-mutilation
- Anorexia
- Bulimia

Behaviour

- Suicide attempts
- Running away
- Depression
- Under-achieving at school
- Over-achieving at school
- Truancy from school
- Without friends/social isolation
- Promiscuity
- Low self-esteem
- Pseudo-adult behaviour
- Homicidal rage attacks
- Drug, alcohol or other substance abuse
- Hysterical attacks
- Staying away from home as much as possible
- Refusal to bring friends home
- Poor concentration at school
- Wary of older person in house
- Compulsive washing of body
- Poor emotional control
- Chronic sense of personal injustice

9 Coping with the crisis

"I just didn't, wouldn't believe her. We were both crying, and I was getting angrier and angrier at her. I kept saying 'tell me it isn't true, tell me you are lying.' I kept on and on at her to deny it, but she wouldn't. She said if I wouldn't believe her she would leave home, but that first she would make sure he would never do it to her younger sisters. I wakened up the rest of them and asked them if they believed what she was saying. Then they started to tell me what he had been doing to each of them too."

Mother talking to author, 1987

Disclosure

There are a number of ways in which you may find out that your child or teenager has been or is being sexually abused:

1. You may find your child engaged in sexual activities with the abuser.

2. Your child may show some of the symptoms listed and, when you take her/him to a doctor or hospital, you may have your suspicions confirmed.

3. You may find out because your child decides to ask you if a particular activity was OK by you, or even because your child decides to tell you that something bad is happening in his/her life.

4. Your child's teacher may notice that s/he is stressed, then question her/him, call a social worker for advice, and you may then be called to the school to be told of their suspicions.

How you react is important

How you, as non-offending parent(s), react to the discovery will have a powerful effect on the outcome of the trauma. There is no doubt that you have a crisis on your hands. If you can handle it in a calm and constructive way, then the short-term and long-term effects of the experience will almost certainly be reduced.

It is as well to understand, right from the moment of discovery, that for the most part you are now on your own.

In the coming months you will have to carry the burden of proof on behalf of your child and, most likely, yourself. You will often find yourself blamed, either subtly or not so subtly, by those to whom you turn for help.

You will almost certainly blame yourself for not protecting your child more. And you may find yourself unable to understand why this has happened, in spite of your care and attention to prevention, and you may want to blame your child also. Try to avoid saying things like: "You should have been more careful." Bear in mind that no child or young person has responsibility for protecting themselves from adults, and cannot be held to blame in any way for what happens to them. Children are powerless against an adult who is determined to abuse or exploit them in any way.

Having to face the possible loss of your child or children, if they are taken into care for their protection, will bring an even greater burden on you. You need help!

You will experience several conflicting emotions, such as disbelief, anger, fear, total despair, guilt, shame. These emotions may be so strong, that for a while you are frozen into inaction.

Choose a good friend for support

For your own sake sit down, with a trusted friend if possible, and look at all the options available to you. Choose one, take a deep breath, and start rebuilding your life.

Remember there are friends and friends. You need one who will allow you to grieve and to express your anger and despair – one you can telephone or call to at any time of the day or night, when anxiety and despair threaten to overwhelm you. At all costs, avoid the friend who gives you advice like "keep your chin up", and who has pat answers to your problems. Such a person may not be able to handle emotional crises themselves very well, despite their ability to project a strong "I am in control of the situation" image.

Immediate short-term strategy

The immediate short-term situation can be traumatic – more traumatic, for some children, than the actual abuse.

If the abuser is your partner, you have to cope with a growing sense of betrayal on two levels: your own and your child's. However, following discovery, you can cope constructively in the short-term by following a few guidelines.

You need to take a number of firm decisions, to protect yourself and your child at this stage.

DON'T

- Panic. If your child sees you getting angry or upset, it may frighten them into complete silence, and they will regret telling you.
- Relentlessly question your child about what has happened.
- Discuss events with friends or relatives in front of the child.
- Talk about ''hanging him'' or mention prison in front of the child.

DO

- Tell your child that you believe her/him.
- Tell your child that you are sorry for what has happened.
- Tell your child that s/he was in no way to blame for what has happened.
- Reassure your child repeatedly that they were absolutely right to tell you about what happened, and that you are glad they did.

- Let your child talk to you about their experience – talking can be therapeutic for both of you.

- Be extremely patient. S/he may begin to exhibit some distress symptoms such as wetting or soiling the bed, or masturbating. With time, support and love, most of these symptoms will disappear, particularly if you listen to the child, and allow her/him to talk about events.

Reassure your child

Reassure your child, again and again, that s/he was right to tell you, that s/he was in no way whatever to blame, that you are going to support them and stop what is happening to them. Avoid at all costs threatening prison, or killing the abuser, since this may serve to create intense anxiety in the child, who may then retract what they have told you, in order to keep their father or brother or uncle out of prison. It can be an unbearable responsibility for a child to feel that they are to be the cause of someone going to prison.

Curb your emotions in front of your child

You will feel often overwhelming rage and anger at the rape and abuse of your child. Why shouldn't you? It is devastating blow to you as a parent. Shock and grieving are normal.

However, remember that the emotions you are feeling – anger, stress, anxiety – may not be the same as your child's. It is quite probable that your child told you in order to get you to stop the unpleasant experience. Once that has stopped, the child may feel an enormous sense of relief. However, if s/he sees that you are deeply upset by what you have been told, they may refuse to talk about the experience again to avoid further upsetting you.

It may be necessary for the child to talk over the experience with a person trained in assessing the possible short and long-term damage which has been done. This is a process called validation. The more your child can talk about the experience, the more control s/he will gain over it. Talking is therapeutic.

Validation

> "Those who are inclined not to believe the child's disclosure fall into two broad camps. Those in the Freudian tradition hold the view that children can and do fantasise about sexual activity with adults, particularly small girls with their fathers.
>
> Another, less defined group, would put forward something probably best described as the 'Salem trial' theory, that is that children can and do make up preposterous stories condemning adults, and cling to them with conviction.
>
> The opposite view, that of most of the people dealing with diagnosis, is simply that children cannot invent in explicit detail, nor relate with such distress, the forms of sexual experience they disclose."
>
> Mary Maher, *Irish Times* 16/7/87

Validation is a relatively new science, begun in Canada and the United States. Prior to its introduction, it was extremely difficult to tell whether a young child was being sexually abused or not. In fact, a complaint of child sexual abuse was usually investigated by an internal examination of the child by a doctor or police surgeon. If the hymen was found intact, then the assumption was that no abuse had taken place. We now know that most children are exposed to a much wider range of sexual activities with adults than sexual intercourse, and one of the positive points of validation is its ability to establish exactly what the child's experience was.

If possible, make an immediate appointment to take your child to a hospital or clinic where validation is carried out. Your social worker or doctor will advise you on this. You may find you have to wait a considerable time for an appointment, but you can use the intervening time to organise yourself, support your child and get protection.

Don't wait to begin protecting yourself and your child until after you have taken your child for validation. All validation will do is to confirm for you that in the opinion of the trained assessor, your child has indeed been sexually abused.

Be ready for negative reactions

Many adults, even those who have trained as doctors, social workers, psychologists, psychiatrists and police officers, react with horror and disbelief at the very suggestion that the child asking them for help and protection has really been sexually abused. Their disbelief may be masked by a professional coldness when dealing with you, a tendency to play down the situation, to offer to talk to the abuser named by the child so that "things can be sorted out". You may find that a barrier is thrown up between you and the agencies which can offer you help. Or you may be swiftly referred to a voluntary agency such as Parents Under Stress or one of the Rape Crisis Centres.

In like manner your family, friends and neighbours may be unable to cope with your trauma, and may rebuse help and support. Use the helplines available (Samaritans, Parents Under Stress, Society for Prevention of Cruelty to Children etc) to keep you going at this time, if necessary. Try to get immediate referral for counselling for yourself so that you have someone to whom you can express your own despair and anger, who understands and sympathises.

Calling a social worker

Social workers are in the front line for every possible community problem. In Ireland at present, there is approximately one available for every 4000 children. Most of them are stretched beyond their limits, but neverthless you may find that they can give you advice, help and support in the initial crisis. Call your local Health Board and explain your situation, and ask to see your local social worker as soon as possible. If you need money to get you or your child to counselling sessions, speak to the senior social worker, and ask for a travel subsidy.

Do you need a barring order?

If the abuser is your partner, you may need to get a barring order immediately, in order to protect you and your child. This can be done in a relatively short period (3 weeks), and has the advantage of giving you breathing space while you sort things out. If you have a solicitor, contact her/him immediately for advice. Be specific about the problem.

Ask for immediate help in getting a barring order, because of possible danger to you and the child. If you decide to take no protective action such as a barring order, you may find that your children will be put into protective care.

Keeping the victim and abuser separated

One of the interesting factors thrown up by the Cleveland case in the summer of 1987 was that so many children were removed from their homes, on discovery of sexual abuse, by social workers. It is a rule of procedure in other countries that when child sexual abuse has been discovered in a family, the child and abuser should be separated immediately. It is recognised that once a child has revealed what is happening, s/he is in danger from the abuser, who may try to intimidate her/him into retracting the disclosure. Indeed, a common experience is for all the family to put pressure on the victim to retract, even to the point of accusing her or him of lying. Children have been put out of their homes for disclosure, or have been committed to institutions until they learned the error of their ways.

However to focus on removing a victim from the family home is ultimately to revictimise that child. The child will have paid a high price for telling, losing family, home and friends. I quote here in full Priniciple 5 of a Statement of Principles produced by the Toronto Metropolitan Chairman's Special Committee on Child Abuse (1982). It is a clear analysis of what often happens when a disclosure is made and should form the basis of any case conferences held about sexually abused children.

Traditional response to child sexual abuse has involved either removing the child from the home or leaving the child and adult together "under supervision". Both actions, however, serve only to further victimise the child, either by isolating her from home, family and friends or by exposing her to continuing risk of abuse.

The primary goals of community intervention are to protect the child from further abuse and to reconstruct a safe, healthy environment for that child. Removal of the offender is the most effective assurance to these ends. It separates the child and offender, thus preventing continued sexual abuse or harassment and, secondly it provides an opportunity for strengthening the relationship between the child and mother. It is the quality of this relationship which has been demonstrated to have a major effect on the child's response and recovery.

Since the majority of sexual abuse cases are not currently criminally prosecuted, the ability to restrict the movements of offenders has been limited. By default, it is then the child victim alone who must face the consequences of disclosure, usually physically or emotionally separated from her family and friends. In choosing to violate a child, surely it is the adult, not the child, who abdicates his rights to home and family, at least temporarily.

The police, child welfare and legal authorities must continue to work together to ensure that sexually abused children are not revictimised by the systems designed to protect them.

The Statement of Principles is reproduced in full in Chapter 12, ''Agenda for Action''.

Access to the victim

If you obtain a barring order, the court may rule that, despite the fact that the order has been given on the grounds of sexual abuse, your partner must have access to his child or children. Sometimes there is an order that access must be supervised, without specifying who should perform this function.

It is becoming increasingly apparent that a growing number of children are continuing to be abused during such "access" visits, even where supervision exists, and mothers should be particularly alert to signs of this, on their children's return. If you have any doubts whatever, speak to the probation officer of the court, or your solicitor, and seek to return to court to have access cut off. There is a certain ambivalence on the part of professionals where access is concerned, on the grounds that "the child wants to see her/his father". This should not be one of the criteria used in deciding whether or not a child should continue to see her/his abuser.

"I objected to him having any access to her at all, but the judge said that he had the right to see his child. He was to see her every Saturday afternoon, and he was to be supervised by his sister. Well, I get on well with his sister - we used be great friends until all this happened – and at first she went along every time, bringing her own son as well for my little one to play with. After a while she stopped going, and just sent her young son along. Now, we find out that he is being sexually abused by my husband as well, and he is still interfering with my daughter. I don't know where to turn. When I said I was not letting her visit him again, his solicitor wrote to me telling me he would take me to court for contempt. So the situation now is that, legally, he can continue to abuse not only my daughter, but his nephew as well.''

Mother of 3-year-old talking to author, 1987

Involving the police

Should you call the police? Any older person who uses a child for his/her own sexual purposes is committing a crime. Legal intervention will serve to make that person understand that what has happened is unacceptable both to you and to society at large. Would you call the police if someone stole your child's bike, or beat your dog? Or damaged your car? Not to call the police in the case of a sexually abused child is to tolerate a criminal activity within your home which is damaging you and your family.

More significantly, some abusers, unless stopped through legal intervention, are quite likely to simply move away from the area and begin again somewhere else.

For many non-abusing parents, and their children, the reality is, however, that they simply cannot take on the further burden of committing the abuser to prison. In the course of my research over the past three years, many victims have said, particularly where their abuser was their father, that they were unable, psychologically and emotionally, to shoulder the guilt of such an action. Their fears, for the most part, rested in their unresolved conflict that they were in some way responsible for what happened. Lack of support following disclosure, which frequently resulted in their removal from the home to be placed in care, only served to convince them that they were the guilty ones, and not the abuser.

If the abused child is a teenager, they should always be involved in any decision on whether or not to involve the police. They are old enough to understand both the nature of the offence, and the implications of reporting or not reporting, and it is a decision they should be allowed to take. Whatever the decision is, they must then be supported fully by you.

If you decide to make a complaint to the police, they will want to talk with your child. In Dublin, at the Sexual Assault Treatment Unit, it is possible to have a policewoman present when the child is being validated. The validation is videotaped, to prevent the child being interviewed continously by the various agencies which will be involved.

However, if you are not near a validation centre, then ask the police to interview you and your child in your home. Stay with your child throughout the interview. If your child uses language which the police may misinterpret, then you should explain as you go along that "that word is the one s/he uses for so and so". Have a friend (or better still, your solicitor) with you at this time, and, if possible, tape record the whole interview. Make sure you get a written statement of your complaint from the police at a later date. Check it with your tape recording to make sure that no important facts were omitted. If they were, write to the police pointing this out.

Once you have made your statement to the police, they will then interview the alleged abuser and any other relevant witnesses, prepare a file, and forward this to the Director of Public Prosecutions.

Waiting for the DPP's decision

All this takes an inordinate amount of time, and it would be unwise to depend on a swift outcome in order to get protection through the legal process for either yourself or your family. Most cases take up to a year to prepare before the DPP can make a decision on whether to prosecute. He is unlikely to do so unless he feels that he can win, because unless the abuser pleads guilty the child will have to go through with the trauma of cross examination in a courtroom, filled with men and women dressed in wigs and gowns, sitting on high platforms, and usually looking very forbidding altogether.

Under these circumstances many children are intimidated, becoming scared, forgetful, and stressed at seeing their abuser often sitting quite close to them in court. If the abuser happens to be their father, then their distress can be so acute that they will be unable to concentrate at all, and the case will be lost.

Look after yourself

There are a number of organisations, which can offer you support and/or conselling, such as:

Parents Under Stress
Rape Crisis Centres
Irish Society for Prevention of Cruelty to Children

(See Appendix A for full list).

Many people believe that therapists or counsellors are all-powerful and immune to the feelings and fears of the rest of the population However, it is important to recognise that although they are people who have professional skills and training, they have experienced the same socialisation that everyone else has. Therefore your intuition and instincts are important factors when selecting a therapist. Therapy should be a participatory process and not the nightmare described so aptly in Sarah Nelson's excellent book, *Incest: Fact and Myth:*

A dense jungle of jargon threatens to overwhelm. There is homeostasis and feedback circularity, there is over-involvement and disequilibrium, there is paradox and incongruity, and there are diagrams with arrows. Scribbled beside the arrows are abbreviations for each family member, Fa-Do-Mo, which sound like the latest Italian soap opera. Lay people have no chance of sharing this knowledge: only an expert can sort the problem out.

Therapists tend to resort to gobbledygook when unsure of their ground or when adopting a non-neutral stance, which is likely to ultimately further undermine your position and role in the family. If you have a Rape Crisis Centre near you, check to see if they run counselling courses for non-abusing parents. If they don't, they may offer you individual counselling. You may find your anger threatening to overwhelm you, so that talking it over with a professional who understands the nature of rape and sexual abuse will be of enormous benefit.

If you were yourself a victim of sexual abuse in childhood you will find this a particularly painful time. Many adults have repressed their early childhood traumas, in order to get on with their lives, and to see the pattern of abuse repeated with their own children can indeed be devastating. If this is the case for you, you should consider breaking silence with an appropriate counsellor at a rape or incest group, to enable you to cope better with your child's abuse.

> "I couldn't believe what I was hearing. My beautiful daughter was telling me that my son, my son!, was raping her, and had been since she was 10 years old. What sort of parents are we that we have raised, using exactly the same family values for both of them, both a victim and a rapist?"

Parents talking to author, 1987

If you are referred to a child and family centre, or a child guidance clinic, beware of efforts , subtle or otherwise, to make you, the non-offending parent, take responsibility for your child's sexual abuse. Should it be suggested that you have been negligent in your parenting, point out firmly that you did not sexually abuse your child, that your family did not sexually abuse your child, and that the only person who has responsibility for this is the abuser. It is important to remind yourself of this, frequently, since a great number of people will need to find a scapegoat other than the actual abuser.

Long-term effects on the victim

The recovery process for most children is slow and painful. You can help it in a number of ways:

- Be patient with wide mood swings and persistent depression. Reassure your child that such emotions are to be expected, and that they will diminish in time.
- Encourage physical activity such as cycling, swimming or hill walking. It may not initially be your child's idea of fun, but getting out in the world again, protected, is of vital importance.
- Don't insist on their participation in social activities such as discos or parties. It could be some time before your child feels self-confident enough to become involved again at this level.
- Offer your child sympathy, a hug, and reassurance that s/he need not forever be fearful of relationships, that what has happened to them is not their fault.

If you have managed to get your child counselling, it may be necessary for her/him to return at intervals over the coming years, since some victims experience apparently irrational phobias and fears intermittently.

The effects on your other (non-abused) children

The disclosure that a father is sexually abusing one of his children can have a depressing effect on the other children, even where support and love is offered by them to the victim. For many sons, their role model has suddenly been identified as the sort of adult they don't want to become. Others, also bonded closely to their father, interpret his behaviour as being within the bounds of male authority, and they may themselves turn to sexual abuse either within or outside the home. One victim told me that her father used to bring in his sons to watch while he was abusing her and her sisters, telling them that when they were older they had the "right" to use their sisters when they wanted to. In time, all the sisters were abused by their brothers, and five of them finally ran away from home, ending up homeless.

Several agencies are establishing therapy groups for the siblings of victims, where their confusion and anger can be discussed in a supportive environment, with others experiencing the same difficulties. As usual, there are not enough such groups available, but call the NSPCC or local Rape Crisis Centre for further information.

Your local community reaction

You may find yourself being ostracised by your neighbours. This can be deeply upsetting, and should never happen, since your neighbours may not know themselves whether their own children have been or are being or will be sexually abused by someone.

It is a common occurrence that if the abuser lives outside your home, but in your community (say a local babysitter), the community, unable to face the reality of what has happened to your children, and the fear that it might have happened to theirs too, frequently comes together to *protect* the abuser. You may be told your child is lying, that you are lying, that you did the abusing yourself, that you brought disgrace and shame on the area.

Try not to despair too much. Support will be found outside the community, through relatives, friends or agencies such as Parents Under Stress. In time, it is possible that common sense will prevail, and your neighbours will rally.

If your child is being harassed by other children in school, speak firmly to the teachers there, pointing out the facts to them. Ask them to introduce a preventive education programme such as Kidscape, into the school, to protect other children (See Appendix C for details). Many Rape Crisis Centres also run such courses for adolescents in schools. However, it is important that parents are involved when such programmes are planned, so that the preventive education is consistent with that being pursued in the home.

Treating the sexual abuser

Since most sexual abuse is a by-product of the society in which we are all reared, it is difficult to know *what* to treat.

Several therapies are offered, depending on who you go to. I deal with some of these in Chapter 10. Few of them, however, address the central issue: that to sexually abuse a child is a criminal offence, and that the adult who has involved the child sexually has abused his/her position of power and trust over that child.

If the abuser is your son, and you resort to a child psychologist or psychiatrist for an explanation of your child's behaviour, you may well be told that his behaviour is "perfectly normal for a child of his age". This reaction raises several questions about the fundamental approach of many such professionals to deviant behaviour in adolescence. In situations such as these, your own common sense should prevail over professional advice, because without skilled help or legal intervention the outcome frequently is that the adolescent abuser grows into an adult rapist, destroying the lives of many innocent people before being caught, if ever.

The reality is that there are few, if any, successful therapies available for treating either the adult or the adolescent abuser. Prison, while it is an imperfect solution, at least has the abuser removed from society for a while, thereby offering protection to a vulnerable section of the community. For some, the reality of prison brings home the seriousness of what they have been doing. For others, there is little or no hope.

10 Who is to blame?

> "If this culture considered it unmasculine for men to want sexual or romantic relationships with partners who are not their equals – partners who are younger, more innocent, vulnerable, less powerful, deferential, and uncritical – then the prevalence of child sexual abuse would also be likely to decline. It would probably decline even more if fathers shared the task of rearing their children equally with mothers, if males were raised with a more nurturing and responsible attitude toward children, and if the family were an institution in which equality existed between male and female adults as well as male and female children."
>
> Diana Russell, *Sexual Exploitation*

While it is important to acknowledge that each of us carries a reservoir of forgotten childhood experiences which inevitably have a bearing on our adult behaviour, this does not absolve us from accountability for our personal choices. I know of no study where a sexual molester has ever admitted and expressed regret about what he was doing before he was detected. Even after discovery he continues to mentally bob and weave in an effort to protect his "good name". He works his way through a range of responses which begin with outright denial of any such behaviour and end with denial to the effect that, although he did behave in this way, he was in no way responsible for his actions.

The progression of denial used by offenders following detection

1	2	3	4	5	6
Denial	*Minimise*	*Justify*	*Mentally ill*	*Self-pity*	*Denial*

1. Denial: perpetrator expresses outrage, hurt, anger.
2. Minimise: "I only did it once – I didn't harm her/him."
3. Justify: see Sarah Nelson's list in Chapter 3.
4. Mentally Ill: "Don't call the police. I'm sick and need treatment."
5. Self-pity: "Look at the trouble you've caused me. Why did you tell? Do you want me to go to prison?"
6. Denial: "It's *your* fault. *You* should have stopped me. *You* know I can't stop myself."

There are three approaches to intervention in child sexual abuse:

1. The "dysfunctional family"

The first is used by those professionals who come from the psychiatric or psychological domain, many of whom place responsibility for what has happened on the ''dysfunctional and disorganised family''. Alternatively you may find yourself, spouse and children labelled as a ''chaotic family''. This leaves the way clear to treat the whole family, by encouraging them all (frequently including child victim) to assume responsibility for the sexual assault. This theory does not define what a dysfunctional family is, nor who has not lived in one.

Another shortcoming with this theory is that it assumes that child sexual abuse only takes place within the family. But the facts are that up to 50% of children are sexually abused outside the home. However, since much of the research on this issue was written around incest, almost all the treatment programmes devised are based on collective family responsibility for this ''dysfunction''.

The underpinning of family ''treatment'' is the reuniting of the whole family, regardless of the wishes of the victim or the spouse. There are always two sides to family ''treatment'': – (a) the therapist's and abuser's and (b) the victim's and mother's. Many survivors have told graphically of the outcome of this unresolved conflict.

''The idea that families should be kept together because this is 'right' also underpins many family treatment programmes. However laudable their aims, practitioners must realise that this is not a neutral position. It is what most male offenders want: it is not necessarily what other family members either want or need. They may pay a heavy price for reunification. An alternative view is that the male offender has forfeited his right to any say in the

> matter, since he has already betrayed his family's trust."
>
> Sarah Nelson, *Incest: Fact and Myth*

2. The art of mother-blaming

The second, and most widely used, model for intervention holds the mother to blame.

Almost without exception the writing on incest and child sexual abuse is based on mother-blaming. Emotive and judgemental terms are used to describe how she *failed to protect* her children, how she *abandoned her wifely role* and *colluded* in the sexual abuse of her children.

If, on the other hand, she wasn't too busy abandoning or colluding, then we are told that it was quite likely she was *denying her husband his conjugal rights*. It is disheartening to find this latter theory present in a book published as recently as 1984 and used widely today by many psychiatrists, doctors and social workers.

> "In other cases a man deprived of his conjugal rights may turn to the nearest available source of gratification – a dependent child."
>
> Dr Arnon Bentovim et al,
> *Child Sexual Abuse within the Family*

Being absent from the home is solemnly invoked to brand the working mother, the sick mother and even the dead mother. (In dying, you merely prove what an irresponsible mother you really are!)

If the mother does not suspect that her children are

being sexually abused, or suspects but has no real proof, she has *turned a blind eye* or *abdicated her maternal role*. On the other hand, if she *only* suspects but makes a complaint anyway to the police or social services she is liable to be identified on someone's report as "spiteful" and "using this unfounded charge to get a barring order". The reality is that the personal cost of making that complaint is seldom understood by either the social worker or the police.

According to one esteemed writer and clinical practitioner, the mother who asked her husband to go upstairs late at night to cover up their daughters, "even though she knew that one of them slept nude" was "*intentionally manoeuvering to set up a sexually abusive situation between her children and their father*." Foolish mother! Did she not realise that the man she married, the father of her children, was only waiting for such an opportunity to assault their children?

These theories are of course nonsense, but dangerous too, since based on these teachings, many doctors, psychiatrists, social workers and lawyers are sent out to "help" or "treat" us.

> "In practice they (professionals) apply their energies to ways of dealing with problems that offer the minimum disruption to the existing order – on peril of their jobs."
>
> D. Ingleby,
> *Mental Health and Social Order*

Researcher Diana Russell gets it about right when she asserts that it has been easier to blame mothers than to face the fact that daughters are vulnerable to sexual abuse when they do not have strong mothers to protect them from their own fathers and other male relatives. But mothers should not have to protect their children from their fathers! And a mother's "failure" to protect her children in this way should not be seen as a causative factor in child sexual abuse.

It has been my experience and that of many others that mothers of sexually abused children fall into three categories:

a) Those who are devastated by the discovery of their child's victimisation and who immediately seek help and advice to try and gain protection for themselves and the family.

b) Those who never suspect that their children are being sexually molested, and who frequently can't possibly know unless they are aware of what to look for.

c) Those who find out, and do nothing.

There are many reasons why a mother may choose to do nothing:

- She may herself be the victim of her husband's brutality, and be living in terror of him. To say anything to him about his behaviour may further endanger her and her children.

- She may have already tried to get help from the social service agencies, and failed.

- She may keep quiet because she does not want any of her children taken from her and put into care, while she is left to live alone with this man who batters her.

- Alternatively, if she takes her courage into her hands and goes to the police, and her partner is imprisoned, she is left without financial support, alone, and frequently forced out of her home by neighbours.

- Sadly, she may have been a victim of sexual abuse in her own childhood, and cannot face the fact that this is now happening to her own children. To face their reality means that, perhaps for the first time ever, she will have to admit to herself what happened to her. That prospect, for many mothers, is simply unbearable.

Is it any wonder that some mothers choose to do nothing?

3. Child sexual abuse and the women's movement

The third model for intervention comes through the women's movement, which raised awareness, both nationally and internationally, about the vast numbers of children who were being sexually abused, about the emotional, social and psychological effects of this experience, and about the reasons why men sexually abused.

Rape Crisis Centres all over the world are counselling women in increasing numbers who have been abused by fathers, brothers, uncles, grandfathers, teachers, priests and school bus-drivers. These women, known as "survivors", have told graphically how they were revictimised by a society which put more value on property than on children's lives, and why they have kept silent throughout their years of ordeal.

Their testimony has changed the emphasis from assault by penile penetration to a wide range of sexual abuses which are perpetrated on children.

Therapy in the Rape Crisis Centres is aimed at helping adult victims to understand what has happened to them, and empowering them with sufficient knowledge to protect themselves in future. Primarily victim-oriented, these centres have given many thousands of adults the courage to speak out publicly about the sexual abuse of children. Latterly, they have become the focus for parents desperate for help, advice and support, and to meet this challenge the centres have devised a number of therapeutic groups which meet regularly.

It is sad and painful to read about or listen to the extraordinary lives some of the mothers have had to live, in order to protect themselves and their children: their beatings, their humiliations, their punishment rapes in front of their children, by men who, when challenged in court, could cheerfully state that they were very sorry, and would behave themselves in future.

The survivors have challenged the assumptions of the family therapists, the medical examinations carried out frequently by male, disbelieving and ultimately dismissive doctors and the "treatment" programmes available to child molesters and rapists, and their voices are increasingly being heard and understood.

Is this love or abuse?

If your partner ever does any of these things to you, you may want to consider whether it is love or abuse:

- Tells anti-women jokes, or makes demeaning remarks about women
- Treats you or other women like sex objects
- Gets jealously angry; assumes you would date or have sex with any available male
- Insists you dress more sexy than you want to

- Belittles your feelings about sex or relationships
- Says you're a cold fish; asks if you're against sex; withholds affection or sex
- Insists on unwanted or uncomfortable touch
- Calls you sexual names like "whore" or "frigid"
- Forces you to do things you don't want to do
- Publicly shows interest in other women
- Has relationships with other women after agreeing to go steady with you
- Forces you to have sex with him or others
- Forces you to watch others have sex
- Forces particular unwanted sex acts
- Forces sex after a fight or physical abuse
- Forces sex when you are sick, or when it is dangerous to your health

- Forces sex without birth control when a pregnancy isn't wanted

- Forces sex and hurts you physically

- Is cruel to you – sexually, physically or emotionally

Giny Nicarthy, *Getting Free: A Handbook for Women in Abusive Relationships*

Why victims think they were sexually abused

Between 1984 and 1987 I talked with a great many victims, both those whose abuse had stopped years ago, and those who were still being abused. As part of research I was carrying out for the Irish Council for Civil Liberties, I posed the question "Why do you think this happened to you?". Below I record the answers which many of them made.

> Because I had to sleep in my daddy's bed when we visited him. My brother slept in the other room.
>
> I was missing my father (who had just died) and one of his best friends offered to comfort me – give me a cuddle, you know?
>
> I was a foster-child, a charity child, and there was no woman in the house since my foster-mother died.
>
> I don't think my parents' sex life was very good. He used to say to me "Oh, your mother loves this".
>
> I was available, vulnerable and defenceless.

It always happened when he came in from seeing his girlfriends.

I wish I knew. I feel very guilty and dirty about it.

I was innocent, trusting. I suppose I was vulnerable to someone like him.

He just picked on me. I was a small child physically.

I was a very well-developed child at 11. I think that was it.

Because of my physical disability I can't get off my back without help, so all he had to do was force me to the ground and I was fair game for him and his friends.

He had a split personality, very nice and "grand" outside the house, and a bloody raging beast inside the front door.

Because I let him, I suppose.

I have to use crutches all the time. I couldn't really get away, could I?

I was in the wrong place at the wrong time for many years.

We were too young to stop him.

My mother couldn't read and he used to send us notes telling us to go upstairs and wait for him.

That's what happens to you when you are the youngest in a large family.

11 Notes to an abuser

The discovery that your child (and indeed your friends' or neighbours' children) is being abused by your husband inevitably precipitates a crisis of major proportions for you and your family. One mother, unable to find someone to talk to, wrote notes to her husband, although she never gave them to him. With her permission some of these are reproduced below. They trace her development from a frightened and confused mother to a woman with a growing awareness of personal identity, capable of survival alone.

> On Halloween our neighbour's children called and accused you. My first feelings were disbelief, because you were always so self-righteous and prudish, and I couldn't connect this sort of accusation and your admission with your image. I still can't.
>
> At first I felt pity for you and the list of victims you named, including our daughter. The list included the children of our closest friends over the years. I felt guilty as you claimed you hadn't got enough sex from me. I didn't want more children, and you wouldn't let me use family planning.
>
> Within one hour of these admissions, you severely verbally abused our children, who had stayed out, with my permission, until 1 a.m. I had to stand between you and them for fear of physical assault, and this display on your part made me feel disgust at all the verbal and physical abuse we have had to put up with from you over

the years, so that next morning I told you I wasn't putting up with it any longer. I wanted a separation.

Over the years we have put up with a lot of petty tyranny, belittling and bullying from you – open and concealed.

You belittled my taste in clothes, because I like casual comfortable things.

You belittled my country expressions, saying that they weren't good English.

You were able to persuade us that we were always wrong, when we disagreed with you, even though we knew we were right!

You never called me by my name, except when blaming me for something.

You created your own personal cold war, and in the last two years of it you withdrew completely from the family to the television. I thought your job was getting you down, but when I heard what you had been up to, it explained a lot of the inexplicable things we had been putting up with.

I spoke to our daughter alone at the first opportunity and only then realised the extent and seriousness of what you had been doing. She was so very young when you started – was she really only four years old? She was so helpless and as time went on and you abused her again and again she felt alone and guilty. We talked like sisters over the days that followed, and we watched you go on as though "reformed"! You kept your temper, helped with the washing up for the first time ever, and took up and read your bible whenever you came in from work.

Our daughter's peace of mind was increasingly shattered by your behaviour, as though nothing at all had happened. She couldn't eat, sleep or study. I asked you to leave us for a while until we sorted out our own feelings, but you refused, saying that you had "stopped all that now". I didn't know if I had the right to insist you left, but I needed space desperately to think.

If you cared at all about our daughter's health you would have gone. But you stayed, and continued to manipulate us and tried to soften us up. You finally, reluctantly, left us at the end of November. Oh! the peace and quiet. But you came back for Christmas, bringing presents, though mostly these were for yourself!

We made an appointment with a doctor at a family centre and on that morning you left the house without us, saying you couldn't wait for us to get ready and adding that anyway we were all mad. At the family centre no one except our older son had anything good to say about you.

When we returned home you started packing, saying you would be selling the house immediately. Our daughter reminded you that she could easily have you put in prison, and you calmed down. Later, you took the family car and left, saying you would probably not be back.

My New Year's Eve was spent alone, sad, lonely and confused. I tried to reason out whether my future would be with or without you and set down some arguments.

1. What do I want to live with you for? It was bad while it lasted and much worse than I realised with all this double life beneath the surface.

2. Would you begin to treat me or our daughter as an equal?

3. How could you and I begin communicating? Now, I feel shut in a box when I am with you, saying polite nothings, because to say "real" things provokes a row.

4. How would we survive your guilt feelings? We have endured the consequences of them for years now, without knowing why.

5. How could I respect someone who has been a "phony" all these years, and would still be one only you were found out?

6. I doubt very much if any improvement has taken place in you, whether you really understand the implications of what you have been doing for years. I can't believe you when you say "I am not doing anything to anyone now", because you add "even though I have the opportunity". That last bit seems like a threat.

7. The longer you are away from us the more I feel it is the right and only solution for now. If some marvellous transformation takes place in you, no doubt it will be noticeable.

8. Lastly, I have to live with myself and feel there is some meaning in things. That would just not be possible if you were here.

An addendum to this particular family's story is that a separation is now in force. The children, who have opted not to see their father again, have received individual and group counselling at a Rape Crisis Centre and the mother is carving out a career for herself. Finance is in short supply, but they have survived with dignity and integrity.

It is expected that the victim, now a young adult, will need counselling at intervals for some years to come. But she is aware of this. At those times when her anger at her victimisation is about to spill over, she returns to a counsellor to enable her to cope.

12 Agenda for future action

> Sexual abuse is a problem which incriminates a particular sex – men – a rather uncomfortable fact for many men to deal with. It makes it harder for them to work enthusiastically on this problem and to avoid defensive responses which can transfer blame from the male offenders to the (often) female victims. Since men occupy powerful policy-making positions, the gender politics of sexual abuse can severely hamper effective policies and public action.
>
> David Finkelhor, *Child Sexual Abuse*

The social policies, what few there are, relating to child sexual abuse are woefully inadequate and, for the most part, are concerned with keeping families together, regardless of whether this is the wish of the non-abusing parent or the victims.

The price of keeping the family together is frequently the removal of the victim from home and family to the "care" of a state institution.

The child who has been abused outside the home

receives little or no recognition in these policies.

The laws designed to protect this most vulnerable section of society are so woefully inadequate that the frequent result of invoking them is the revictimisation of the child.

In Ireland and England, at the present time, there are a number of groups looking at the area of social and legal reform. What will become of their reports or recommendations is a matter of public concern. The likelihood is that after an initial flurry of statements, voiced by politicians claiming to be "disturbed" and "concerned" and by church groups agonising about the "rights" of parents over their children, either nothing at all will happen, or it will happen with such a lack of urgency that another generation of children will be sexually abused before political expediency is transformed into action. Children have no votes. Parents have votes.

In the early part of this decade, a special committee on child abuse was established in Toronto, Canada. Members of the group were drawn from the different agencies concerned with the care and protection of children, including religious groups, the Attorney General's Office, Rape Crisis Groups, etc. From their deliberations, which are still continuing, there was developed and implemented a comprehensive response to child sexual abuse, based on seven principles.

I reproduce the document in full, in the hope that it will be read and debated by parents everywhere, and brought to the attention of the policy makers, as an acceptable way forward if we are to confront the problem of child sexual abuse.

Preamble

The sexual abuse of children is a phenomenon which has only recently gained some measure of public and professional attention. With this attention has come both an increase in the number of reported cases and a recognition of the inadequacies of traditional methods of response.

Given the range of professionals who may be called into action upon disclosure of sexual abuse, it is critical that efforts be coordinated. During the past year, the Metropolitan Chairman's Special Committee on Child Abuse has provided an active forum through which relevant issues have been identified, debated and resolved in a collaborative attempt to develop a common understanding of and approach to the problem.

The following principles have emerged through these initial efforts and are designed to provide a framework for a comprehensive response to child sexual abuse. As such, they are not intended to restrict or limit efforts but rather to support attempts to implement a consistent and appropriate response, integrating the best which each responsible system has to offer.

Every situation involving child sexual abuse must be assessed individually to determine the best interests of the child involved. We believe that creative application of the following principles will help to guide us consistently toward that end.

A STATEMENT OF PRINCIPLES

1. ***Children reporting sexual abuse should be presumed to be telling the truth and bear no responsibility for their involvement, regardless of time or circumstances.***

   Reliable estimates suggest that one in four girls and one in ten boys will be sexually molested by an adult at some point in their childhood. Up to 80% of these children will know their molester and, half of the time, he will be their natural or substitute father.*

   Translating the experiences of communities with

considerable success in responding to their problem, it may be estimated that over 3,000 children are sexually abused each year in Metropolitan Toronto. Yet, in 1980, only 501 sexual offences involving children were reported to the police, and the Children's Aid Societies forwarded only 75 verified cases of intra-familial child sexual abuse to the Provincial Child Abuse Registry.

Until recently, effective response to child sexual abuse has been severely hampered by the age-worn myth that children fantasise about sexual encounters with adults. This myth is further complicated by an insidious but equally damaging belief that if, in fact, sexual activity occurs, the child is usually a provocative, if not eager, participant.

Fortunately, adults who were molested as children and experienced professionals are now helping to destroy this ill-conceived and dangerous belief system. Experience clearly demonstrates that children do *not* lie about sexual abuse. In fact, false *denials* of sexual abuse are infinitely more common than false *reports*.

All systems responsible for serving children must recognise the alarming prevalence of sexual abuse and commit themselves to responding, without doubt or delay, if a child comes forward. Without this commitment, the balance of power will remain forever in the hands of those adults who choose to violate the bodies and spirits of children.

2. ***The use of a child by an adult for sexual purposes is an abusive and criminal act which should be investigated and prosecuted as such.***

Any form of direct or indirect sexual contact between a child and an adult is exploitive since it is motivated by adult needs and involves a child who, by virtue of age and position, is unable to give consent.

The closer the relationship between the child and the adult, the greater the potential damage is to the child. It appears that, ultimately, it is the abuse of trust and authority, more than the nature of the sexual contact, which causes the most trauma to the child as she matures. For this reason, father-daughter incest must be viewed most seriously, not simply as a ''family problem'' but also as an abusive situation with potential life-long effects upon the child victim and frequently her siblings.

No adult who molests a child should be exempt, particularly by virtue of family relationship, from accountability for his actions. The sexual abuse of children is a crime which cannot by any measure be tolerated or excused. As such, the community has both the right and obligation to take the necessary steps to protect the child, and to ensure that the adult in question is deterred from any further abusive acts.

Criminal prosecution conveys a clear message to the offender that his behaviour is both legally and morally unacceptable; that he, alone, is responsible for the abuse and its consequences; and that the community is prepared to mobilise its resources to protect children. Finally, it also has the benefit of empowering the child victim who sees that she is believed and comes to understand that the disruption in her family is not her fault but a result of the abuse which was inflicted upon her.

3. ***Conviction of offenders, however, is not enough. Without appropriate treatment, the risk of re-offence remains high.***

The causes of child sexual abuse are the subject of much debate and speculation. It is accepted, however, that the adult's disturbance is deeply-rooted and usually beyond voluntary control. It is not surprising, therefore, that offenders who receive no treatment or who attempt to engage in treatment voluntarily are generally undeterred in their behaviour.

One reputable study, for example, indicated that the vast majority of incarcerated sex offenders were known to authorities prior to conviction. Offender treatment specialists in Seattle, Washington, report further that less than one per cent of offenders remains in treatment on a voluntary basis. There is no reason to assume that the experience in Metropolitan Toronto is significantly different.

Court-ordered treatment offers the best assurance that treatment will, in fact, occur. This, of course, assumes the continued development of offender treatment services which are willing to accept clients who are, at least initially, involuntary.

The engagement of the offender in treatment also helps to reassure the child victim that the offender, who may also be her father, while being punished is also receiving help for his problem. This assurance is particularly important for a child who may be feeling guilty for "breaking up the family" or "sending daddy away or to jail".

4. ***Effective response requires the full co-operation and co-ordination of all systems. Specialisation of core personnel is necessary to promote sensitivity, consistency and collaboration.***

Every child who has been sexually abused is the potential subject of an array of professionals, many of whom may have little or no experience or knowledge of the problem. For example, in the space of several days, a child could be interviewed by a teacher, a public health nurse or school social worker, one or more child welfare workers, several police officers, plus medical and legal personnel. Faced with the constant re-telling of their stories and, quite possibly, conflicting reactions and advice, it is not surprising that many children retreat into silence or deny the truth of their original report.

Given the critical importance of appropriate and sensitive response to disclosure, specific personnel in each system should be designated and trained co-operatively as child sexual abuse specialists. Together this core of inter-disciplinary specialists can develop and refine new procedures and techniques to improve and co-ordinate detection, reporting, investigation and Court involvement, as well as crisis support and treatment for the sexually abused child and her family.

5. ***Following disclosure of sexual abuse, the child victim and adult offender should be separated immediately. In intra-familial situations, every effort should be made to remove the offender from the home, rather than the child.***

Traditional response to child sexual abuse has involved either removing the child from the home or leaving the child and adult offender together "under supervision". Both actions, however, serve only to further victimise the child, either by isolating her from home, family and friends, or by exposing her to continuing risk of abuse.

The primary goals of community intervention are to protect the child from further abuse and to reconstruct a safe, healthy environment for that child. Removal of the offender is the most effective assurance to these ends. It separates the child and offender, thus preventing continued sexual abuse or harassment and, secondly, it provides an opportunity for strengthening the relationship between the child and mother. It is the quality of this relationship which has been demonstrated to have a major effect on the child's response and recovery.

Since the majority of sexual abuse cases are not currently criminally prosecuted, the ability to restrict the movements of offenders has been limited. By default, it is then the child victim alone who must face the consequences of disclosure, usually physically or emotionally separated from her family and friends. In choosing to violate a child, surely it is the adult, not the child, who abdicates his rights to home and family, at least temporarily.

The police, child welfare and legal authorities must continue to work together to ensure that sexually abused children are not re-victimised by the systems designed to protect them.

6. *Attention must be given to the development of specialised crisis and treatment services for the child victim and non-offending family members*

Experts have emphasised that the quality of response in the first 48 hours following disclosure of sexual abuse determines the eventual outcome for the child. Immediate and intensive intervention, coupled with crisis support services, significantly improves the chances for successful resolution of the initial crisis caused by disclosure, as well as for subsequent progress in treatment.

Current services for child sexual abuse victims, particularly those who are involved in Court proceedings, are extremely limited in both scope and number. In fact, the only specialised services which exist are those offered through the Hospital for Sick Children and York-Finch Hospital, both of which are already extended beyond their capacities. While the Children's Aid Societies may attempt to fill this critical gap, they are ill-equipped to provide intensive crisis support and treatment while also trying to investigate and co-ordinate response. Continuing efforts must be made to ensure that appropriate treatment and support services are readily accessible throughout Metropolitan Toronto.

7. ***Early detection and prevention provide the ultimate key to ending the destructive consequences of child sexual abuse.***

Given that most sexual abuse begins when a child is between the ages of five and nine, and continues over a period of years, early detection and prevention are critical. At the present time, probably no more than ten per cent of all sexually abused children come to official attention. Most of these are adolescents, many of whom are already exhibiting serious problems as a result of on-going sexual abuse. Successful intervention becomes more problematic as the abuse continues.

The effects of child sexual abuse can reach far into the future. Those children who are believed and supported have the best chance of growing up whole and healthy. Others must engage in a life-long struggle against repeated victimisation. Some, tragically, carry the lessons learned in childhood to their own children by becoming abusive parents themselves.

While it is critical that services and support be available for current victims of child sexual abuse, it is equally important that efforts promoting early detection and prevention be encouraged. Possible examples include experiential school programs for young children, public education, parent support programs and continuing research aimed at enhanced understanding of the origins and dynamics of child sexual abuse.

No single individual, agency or system, however, can respond in isolation to child sexual abuse. It is a community problem of alarming and destructive proportions. There must be a collective commitment to work together, with all the compromise, frustration and understanding required, to create a community which refuses to tolerate the sexual abuse of its children.

---

* These general estimates are drawn from the results of five major surveys, conducted between 1940 and 1978 including C. Landis (1940), A. Kinsey (1953), J. Landis (1956), J. Gagnon (1965), and D. Finkelhor (1978). Their findings are also supported by the experiences of the Harborview Sexual Assault Center in Seattle, Washington and the Child Sexual Abuse Treatment Program in San Jose, California which, together, have treated over 10,000 sexually abused children in the past decade. Informal surveys in Canada suggest a similar incidence.

Appendix A

List of works consulted

Adams, Carel, J. Fay and J. Loreen-Martin, *NO is Not Enough: Helping Teenagers Avoid Sexual Assault* (Impact Publishers, California, 1985).

Askew, S. and C. Ross, *Anti-Sexist Work With Boys* (Isledon Teachers' Centre/ILEA, 1985).

An Roinn Slainte, *Guidelines on Procedures for the Identification, Investigation and Management of Child Abuse* (Department of Health (Ireland), 1987).

Brownmiller, Susan, Against our Will: *Men, Women and Rape* (Penguin 1986).

Butler, Sandra, *Conspiracy of Silence: The Trauma of Incest* (Volcano Press, 1978).

Casburn, M., *Girls Will Be Girls: Sexism and Juvenile Justice in a London Borough*. Explorations in Feminism No.6 (WRRC Publications, 1979).

Cohen, S. and A. Scull, *Social Control and the State* (1983).

Colao, Flora and T. Hosansky, *Your Children Should Know* (Bobbs-Merrill, 1983).

Elliott, Michele, *Keeping Safe: A Practical Guide To Talking With Children* (Bedford Press, 1986).

Finkelhor, David, *Child Sexual Abuse: New Theory & Research* (The Free Press, 1984).

Fortune, M. M., *Sexual Abuse Prevention: A Study for Teenagers* (United Church Press, New York, 1984).

Godfrey, P. (Chairman), *Child Sexual Abuse Protocol* (The Metropolitan Chairman's Special Committee on Child Abuse, Toronto, 1983).

Graham, B. (Chairman), *Developing A Child Centred Response To Sexual Abuse.* A Discussion Paper. (South-West Region Working Party, 1984).

Irish Times, Jan-July 1987.

Lane, M. E. (Chairman), *The Legal Response to Sexual Abuse of Children* (The Metropolitan Chairman's Special Committee on Child Abuse, Toronto, 1982).

Market Research Bureau of Ireland Limited, *Child Sexual Abuse in Dublin* (Pilot Survey Report, 1987).

Mrazek P., B. Kempe and C. Henry, *Sexually Abused Children and their Families* (Pergamon Press, 1985).

Porter, R., *Child Sexual Abuse within the Family* (CIBA Foundation/Tavistock Publications, 1984).

Nelson, M. and K. Clark, *Preventing Child Sexual Abuse* (Network Publications, 1986).

Nelson, Sarah, *Incest: Fact and Myth* (Stramullion, 1987).

Reisman, J. A., *Children in Playboy, Penthouse and Hustler* (Institute for Media Education, Arlington VA, 1986).

Rogers, C. R., *Client-Centred Therapy* (Constable, 1986).

Russell, Diana, *Sexual Exploitation: Rape, Child Sexual Abuse, and Workplace Harassment* (Sage, 1984).

Sgroi, Susanne, *Handbook of Clinical Intervention in Child Sexual Abuse* (Lexington, 1982).

S.M.A.S.H., *The Pack: an information pack for men* (Sheffield Men Against Sexual Harassment, 1984).

Zilbergeld, B. *Men and Sex* (Fontana, 1978).

The Children's Legal Centre, *Childright* (CLC).

Appendix B

Directory of contacts

Ireland

BATTERED WIVES AND CHILDRENS REFUGES	Athlone (0902) 741 22
	Belfast (084) 662 385
	662 348
	Bray (01) 863 484
	Coleraine (080265) 823 195
	Cork (021) 392 300
	Derry (0504) 265 967
	Dublin (01) 961 002
	Galway (091) 659 85
	Limerick (061) 423 54
	Omagh (0662) 477 46
	Portrush (0265) 823 182
CHERISH (Support and advice for single parents)	Dublin (01) 682 744
INCEST CRISIS SERVICE	Dublin (01) 743 796
IRISH SOCIETY FOR THE PREVENTION OF CRUELTY TO CHILDREN	Dublin (01) 760 423

Currently establishing a 24-hour helpline for parents, children and other family members. Counselling services will be available in late 1987.

PARENTS UNDER STRESS	Dublin (01) 742 066
RAPE CRISIS CENTRES	Belfast (084) 249 696
	Clonmel (052) 241 11
	Cork (021) 968 086
	Dublin (01) 614 911

RAPE CRISIS CENTRES (Contd.)

	Galway (091) 649 83
	Limerick (061) 311 511
	Waterford (051) 733 62
RAPE AND INCEST LINE	Belfast (084) 226 083
SAMARITANS	Ballymena (08494) 435 55
	Belfast (084) 664 422
	Cork (021) 213 23
	Derry (0504) 227 77
	Dublin (01) 727 700
	Ennis (065) 297 77
	Galway (091) 639 89
	Limerick (061) 421 11
	Newry (080693) 663 66
	Omagh (0662) 449 44
	Waterford (051) 721 14

England

BIRMINGHAM RAPE CRISIS CENTRE	(021) 233 2122
BRADFORD RAPE CRISIS CENTRE	(0274) 308 270
BRIGHTON RAPE CRISIS CENTRE	(0273) 203 773
BRISTOL RAPE CRISIS CENTRE	(0272) 428 331
CAMBRIDGE RAPE CRISIS CENTRE	(0223) 358 314
CHILDLINE (FREEPHONE) LONDON	0800-1111
CLEVELAND RAPE CRISIS CENTRE	(0642) 225 787
CORNWALL RAPE CRISIS CENTRE	(0209) 714 407

COVENTRY RAPE CRISIS CENTRE	(0203) 772 29
COVENTRY ONE IN FOUR	(0203) 766 06
CUMBRIA RAPE CRISIS CENTRE	(0228) 365 00
GRAYS THURROCK RAPE CRISIS CENTRE	(0375) 380 609
HARLOW INCEST SURVIVORS CRISIS LINE	(Harlow) 216 12
HULL RAPE CRISIS CENTRE	(0482) 299 90
ISICSA, LONDON	(01) 852 7432
KINGSTON WOMEN'S CENTRE, SURREY	(01) 541 1964
LAMBETH INCEST SURVIVORS, LONDON	(01) 274 7215
LEEDS RAPE CRISIS CENTRE	(0532) 440 058
LIVERPOOL RAPE CRISIS CENTRE	(051) 727 7599
LONDON FAMILY NETWORK	(01) 514 1177
LONDON INCEST CRISIS LINE	(01) 388 2388
LONDON INCEST SURVIVORS CAMPAIGN	(01) 671 9033
LONDON PARENTS ANONYMOUS	(01) 263 8918
LONDON PARENTS UNDER STRESS	(01) 645 0469
LONDON RAPE CRISIS CENTRE	(01) 837 1600
LONDON WOMEN'S THERAPY CENTRE	(01) 263 6200
LUTON FAMILY NETWORK	(0582) 422 751

LUTON RAPE CRISIS CENTRE	(0582) 335 92
MANCHESTER FAMILY NETWORK	(061) 236 9873
MANCHESTER RAPE CRISIS CENTRE	(061) 228 3602
MANCHESTER TABOO CENTRE	(061) 236 1323
NORWICH RAPE CRISIS CENTRE	(0603) 667 687
NOTTINGHAM RAPE CRISIS CENTRE	(0602) 410 440
NSPCC, LONDON	(01) 242 1626
READING RAPE CRISIS CENTRE	(0734) 555 77
ROCHDALE RAPE CRISIS CENTRE	(0706) 526 279
SHEFFIELD INCEST SURVIVORS GROUP	(0742) 755 255
SHEFFIELD RAPE CRISIS CENTRE	(0742) 775 255
SUSSEX INCEST CRISIS LINE	(0273) 243 16
SAMARITANS	see local phone directory

Scotland

ABERDEEN INCEST SURVIVORS GROUP	(0224) 575 560
ABERDEEN RAPE CRISIS CENTRE	(0224) 575 560
DUNDEE RAPE CRISIS CENTRE	(0382) 840 077
DUNFERMLINE RAPE CRISIS LINE	(0383) 739 084

EDINBURGH RAPE CRISIS CENTRE	(031) 556 9437
EDINBURGH SPCA	(031) 337 8539
FALKIRK RAPE CRISIS CENTRE	(0324) 384 33
FALKIRK INCEST SURVIVORS GROUP	(0324) 384 33
GLASGOW FAMILY NETWORK	(041) 221 6722
HIGHLAND RAPE CRISIS CENTRE (INVERNESS)	(0463) 233 089
SAMARITANS	see local phone directory

Wales

CARDIFF & S.E. WALES CPT	(0222) 397146 / 371080 / 378837
FAMILY NETWORK, CARDIFF	(0222) 29461
INCEST HELPLINE	(0222) 733929
RAPE CRISIS CENTRE, CARDIFF	(0222) 373181
SAMARITANS	see local phone directory

Appendix C

Suggestions for further reading

Non-fiction

Brownmiller, Susan, *Against Our Will: Men, Women and Rape* (Pelican).
Cullen, Mary, *Girls Don't Do Honours* (Women's Education Bureau (Ireland)).
Duncan, William, *Children's Rights under the Constitution* (Irish Council for Civil Liberties).
Dworkin, Andrea, *Pornography* (Women's Press).
Ennew, Judith, *The Sexual Exploitation of Children* (Polity).
Forward and Buck, *Betrayal of Innocence* (Pelican).
Hall, R.E., *Ask Any Woman* (Falling Wall).
Jackson, Stevi, *Childhood and Sexuality* (Blackwell).
Kempe and Kempe, *Child Abuse* (Fontana).
London Rape Crisis Centre, *Sexual Harassment: The Reality for Women* (LRCC).
Masson, John, *The Assault on Truth* (Faber).
Miller, Alice, *Thou Shalt Not Be Aware* (Pluto).
Nelson, Sarah, *Incest: Fact and Myth* (Straumullion).
Rush, Florence, *The Best Kept Secret* (Prentice-Hall).
Russell, Diana, *Sexual Exploitation: Rape, Child Sexual Abuse and Workplace Harassment* (Sage).
Sereny, Gitta, *The Invisible Children* (Pan).
SMASH, *The Pack* (Information pack for men on sexual harassment, rape and sexual abuse of children) (Lifespan, Dunfort Bridge, Yorkshire).
Stones, Rosemary, *Too Close Encounters and What to do About Them* (Methuen).
Sweetman, Rosita, *On Our Backs: Sexual Attitudes in a Changing Ireland* (Pan).
Turner, Janine, *A Crying Game* (Mainstream).
Ward, Elizabeth, *Father-Daughter Rape* (Women's Press).

Fiction/biography

Angelou, Maya, *I Know Why the Caged Bird Sings* (Women's Press).
Butler, Sandra, *Conspiracy of Silence* (Volcano Press).
Chick, Sandra, *Push Me, Pull Me.* (Women's Press).
Irwin, Hadley, *A Girl Like Abbey* (Kestrel).
McNaron and Morgan, *Voices in the Night* (Cleis Press).
Nelson, Dorothy, *In Night's City* (Wolfhound).
Spring, Jacqueline, *Cry Hard and Swim: The Story of an Incest Survivor* (Virago).
Walker, Alice, *The Color Purple* (Women's Press).

Select list of non-sexist children's reading

2 – 7 YEARS

Ahlberg, A., *Happy Families Series* (Puffin).
Aliki, *Feelings* (Piccolo Picture Books).
Browne, Anthony, *Piggy book* (Magnet).
Hollick, Helen, *Come and Tell Me* (Dinosaur Books).
Hughes, Shirley, *Sally's Secret* (Puffin).
McAafee, A, *Visitors Who Came To Stay* (Hamish Hamilton).
Mahy, Margaret, *Man Whose Mother was a Pirate* (Puffin).
Ormorod, Jan, *Sunshine* (Puffin).
Ormorod, Jan, *Moonlight* (Puffin).
Sendak, Maurice, *Sign on Rosie's Door* (Puffin).
Stewart, Anne, *The Bus Driver (Hamish Hamilton).*
Stewart, Anne, *The Ambulance Woman* (Hamish Hamilton).
Storr, Catherine, *Polly and the Wolf Again* (Puffin).
Vesey, Ann, *The Princess and the Frog* (Magnet).

Wells, Rosemary, *Morris's Disappearing Bag* (Puffin).
Winthrop, Elizabeth, *Sloppy Kisses* (Puffin).
Yeoman, J and Q. Blake, *The Wild Washerwomen* (Puffin).

8 – 11 YEARS

Bawden, Nina, *Carrie's War* (Puffin).
Bawden, Nina, *Peppermint Pig* (Puffin).
Bradman, Tony, *Through My Window* (Methuen).
Corballis, Judy, *The Wrestling Princess & Other Stories* (Knight).
Kemp, Gene, *The Turbulent Term of Tyke Tyler* (Puffin).
Kilner, Geoffrey, *The Bright Key* (Methuen).
Miller, M.L, *Dizzy From Fools* (Neugebauer Press).
Murphy, Jill, *The Worst Witch* (Puffin).
Williams, Jay, *The Practical Princess* (Hippo).

YOUNG ADULTS

Ashley, Bernard, *Running Scared* (Puffin).
Greene, Bette, *Summer of my German Soldier* (Puffin).
Guy, Rosa, *Edith Jackson* (Puffin).
Hautzig, Esther, *The Endless Steppe* (Puffin).
Kennemore, Tim, *The Fortunate Few* (Puffin).
Leggett, J & Blatchford, R. *It's Now or Never* (Bell & Hyman).
Stones, Rosemary, *More to Life than Mr Right* (Fontana).
Ure, J., *A Proper Little Nooreyeff* (Puffin).

Various Authors: *Mad and Bad Fairies* (Attic Press).
Ms Muffet and Others (Attic Press).
Rapunzel's Revenge (Attic Press).

Video for parent/teacher use

Kidscape have produced an extremely well-researched video programme for use in schools, involving parents and teachers, which has been widely and successfully used throughout the UK. Details are available from: **Kidscape,** 82 Brook Street, London W1Y 1YG. Telephone 493 – 9845